his name
was death

Other titles available in Vintage Crime/Black Lizard

By Fredric Brown

The Far Cry

By David Goodis

Black Friday

The Burglar

Nightfall

Shoot the Piano Player

Street of No Return

By Richard Neely

Shattered

By Jim Thompson

After Dark, My Sweet

The Getaway

The Grifters

A Hell of a Woman

The Killer Inside Me

Nothing More Than Murder

Pop. 1280

By Charles Willeford

The Burnt Orange Heresy

Cockfighter

Pick-Up

By Charles Williams

The Hot Spot

his name
was death

fredric brown

VINTAGE CRIME / **BLACK LIZARD**

vintage books • a division of random house, inc. • new york

First Vintage Crime/Black Lizard Edition, July 1991

Library of Congress Cataloging-in-Publication Data
Brown, Fredric, 1906–1972.
His name was death/Fredric Brown.
p.   cm. —(Vintage crime/Black Lizard)
"Originally published by E. P. Dutton & Co., Inc. in 1954"—T.p. verso.
ISBN 0-679-73468-6
I. Title.   II. Series: Vintage Crime/Black Lizard.
PS3505.R8135H55   1991
813'.54—dc20   90-50590   CIP

Manufactured in the United States of America
10 9 8 7 6 5 4 3 2 1

his name
was death

Her name was Joyce Dugan, and at four o'clock on this February afternoon she had no remote thought that within the hour before closing time she was about to commit an act that would instigate a chain of murders.

She was a pretty girl. Five feet three, a hundred and ten well distributed pounds. Fair skin, as clear and smooth as a baby's. Smoothly wavy hair, blonde and in a long bob. Slightly turned-up nose with just a few faint freckles on and around it. A mouth that looked kissable, and was.

Dainty hands as fast as little white mice as they folded handbills on the counter at which she stood.

She wore a short-sleeved linen frock that was still white and crisp at the end of a busy day. She made a pretty picture working there; unfortunately, there was no one to see it. She was alone in the little printing shop on Santa Monica Boulevard. Mr. Conn, the man who ran the shop, had left a little early that day, just fifteen minutes ago.

Outside, it had finally decided not to rain and the sun, which had been hiding behind clouds all day, now shone brightly as it headed downward toward the ocean just beyond the end of the boulevard.

Joyce looked longingly through the not-too-clean glass of the door and windows at that sunshine and wished that the next hour were done. Looked down at the pile of unfolded handbills and wondered whether she'd be able to finish them in an hour. Just about, she decided, if she worked fast. She hoped so, because she hated working overtime and these had to be finished. The man for whom they'd been printed would be in at five to get them and if they weren't ready yet, she'd have to keep him waiting and work overtime herself. Every minute after five o'clock was on her own time and was precious.

Not that Mr. Conn often asked her to work overtime, at least not more than a few minutes or so to finish anything she was working on that had to be finished that day. The few times that she'd worked *real* overtime, several hours, he'd always added something to her pay even though she was on straight salary and wasn't docked when, on occasion, she missed a day or so. And he'd given her a week's vacation with pay only a month ago, although she'd worked for him only eight months then and didn't really have a vacation coming yet, when she'd had a chance to go to Los Padres for skiing and ice skating with two girl friends of hers who were driving there. Yes, she thought Mr. Conn was a creep in some ways but he was generous and considerate in others. Before he'd left this afternoon, for instance, he'd asked her if she was sure she could finish that folding by five; he'd have stayed and given her a hand for a while otherwise. She hoped she hadn't been too optimistic in assuring him that she could do it easily.

Especially because this was Friday and working over on Friday seemed worse than any other day of the week, with Saturday and Sunday coming up, the two-day week end.

That was one reason why she liked this job so much better than her last one, clerking in a department store. Stores have to keep open on Saturday; it's their biggest day. With a printer it doesn't matter; he'd probably do less business on Saturday than on other days.

Another reason why she liked this job was the fact that it wasn't all doing the same thing over and over; it had variety and that made time go a lot faster than when you did just one thing all day long as you do in most store or office jobs. Mr. Conn did all the skilled work, the printing and engraving (although he didn't get much engraving to do). And she, Joyce, did just about everything else. She took his letters and did the bookkeeping despite the fact that she wasn't really fully qualified as either a stenographer or bookkeeper; the letters to be written were so few and the bookkeeping so simple that she had no trouble with either. And she did folding and wrapping and all sorts of other jobs.

Folding she liked better (or at least disliked less) than any other kind of work, because it left her mind free to think and to dream. Her fingers did it automatically once they were started, and her thoughts were free to roam wherever they wanted.

And thank Heaven her thoughts were tending more and more to roam to pleasant things and not to grieving over

Joe. Each day now she found herself thinking less and less about him and she told herself that was as it should be. The one year she'd been married to Joe Dugan had been the happiest year of her life and she'd probably never be that happy again. But he'd died sixteen, almost seventeen months ago and even Joe wouldn't want her to spend the rest of her life grieving over him. He'd say, "Jeez, honey, a dish like you wasting yourself? And only twenty-three! Get in there and pitch. I'm not the only pebble on the beach." That's what Joe would tell her if he was here. But, of course, if he was here—

She sighed, looked at the clock again, and tried to make her fingers go even faster on the folding.

Yes, it was time she thought about Joe less and less except as a wonderful memory (and he'd always be that) and tried to find someone else she could love and with whom she could be whole again.

She'd tried. That week at Los Padres she'd tried, tried so hard to let herself feel attracted to the young man with the sleek black hair who was such a good dancer, but she just couldn't. Not someone like him, and he'd probably just been making passes anyway.

She sighed and looked at the clock again.

Tomorrow, Saturday, would be a plenty busy day, looking for a new room and getting moved into it, all in the same day. Moving, in any case, to a hotel if she didn't find a room that would do in a rooming house. She wished now that she hadn't had that argument with Mrs. Prescott, her landlady—although it had been all Mrs. Prescott's fault and Joyce had tried to be reasonable with her—and given notice. But she had given notice and Mrs. Prescott had been so nasty about it all week that she just couldn't try to withdraw the notice now and stay longer. She *had* to find a room tomorrow, or go to a hotel and that would mean having to move twice.

But after she moved she'd start getting out more, going to dances, things like that. Places where she had at least a chance of meeting some nice men, ones she could like. That was the only trouble with working in such a little printing shop as this one; she met almost nobody through her work. When Mr. Conn was in he always went to the front and talked to the customers who came in, and Mr. Conn was in almost all of the time. She got to know only the few very regular customers and those of Mr. Conn's friends who dropped in once in a while. And they were all men too old for her, almost twice her age most of them. Not that some of them weren't likable enough—especially that friend of Mr. Conn's, Charlie Barrett, who was a sergeant on the Santa Monica detective force. He always took time to talk to Joyce and kid around with her, but in a nice way. Too old for her, though, like all the others, and anyway he hadn't been in recently. Or like Mr. Gutzmer who'd be in at five for these handbills she was folding. He was nice too, but.

A ringing bell told her that the door had just opened but before turning toward it she glanced up at the clock again. Ten minutes to five. Well, if it was Mr. Gutzmer for his handbills, he was early and she still had a good ten minutes' work on them; he'd have to wait.

Then she turned toward the door and saw that it wasn't Mr. Gutzmer.

It was a tall, broad-shouldered young man with red hair and a grin. And she knew him, but she couldn't place him for just a second. He was looking at her with the same slightly puzzled look that must be on her own face. Then she placed him.

"Claude Atkins," she said wonderingly.

"Joyce!" He had it too now. He came forward to the counter and leaned on it. "Where've you been all these years?"

"Around," she said.

All these years. Five years at least—no, six. No wonder they hadn't recognized one another right away. She'd been seventeen and he'd been eighteen when they'd known one another in high school. He'd graduated a year sooner than she and they'd drifted apart; she thought he'd probably gone somewhere. And she'd met Joe Dugan and had forgotten that she'd once thought she was in love with Claude Atkins.

"My God, but you've grown up to be pretty, Joyce," he said.

She laughed. "You've grown up too, Claude." And changed for the better, she thought. The six years between eighteen and—he'd be twenty-four or twenty-five now—do make a lot of difference. He'd been a boy then and he was a man now, not exactly a handsome man but an awfully attractive one. And for him of all people to walk in Mr. Conn's shop just when she'd been thinking what she'd just been thinking!

"Gee, it's swell to see you again. Say, is Mr. Conn in?"

She shook her head. "He went home a little over an hour ago. Anything I can do for you?"

He laughed, "A leading question if I ever heard one. But didn't Conn say anything about me, leave anything for me?"

Joyce shook her head again. "No, he didn't. Was he supposed to have?"

"He sure was. He was going to give me some money today. You positive he isn't coming back?"

"Positive, Claude. He must have forgotten. But I handle all the bookkeeping and I didn't know—What was it for?"

"It wasn't business. Not printing business, anyway. We swapped cars last night."

"Swapped *cars*?"

He chuckled. "Yeah, in a tavern. Sounds crazy, but it wasn't. We were each having a drink and got to talking about cars and I said I liked convertibles. He said he had one and wished he had something else and I said I'd swap him a sedan for it. I thought I was kidding because my car was a forty-one and I thought his would probably be worth plenty more. But it turned out his convertible was a forty-one too, and we both had our cars parked outside so we went out and looked at them and tried them out."

"And traded, just like that?"

"Pretty much just like that. Oh, we dickered a while. Mine was in a hell of a lot better shape than his. His needed some new canvas and plenty other work, including a ring job. I can fix it myself—I'm a mechanic—but it'll take a lot of my time and some money for parts. I wouldn't have traded even. But we settled for his paying me ninety bucks difference.

"We signed over the papers right there but he didn't have that much cash or a checkbook with him so he said if I came by here late this afternoon he'd give me the ninety bucks in cash and finish the deal."

"Gee, Claude, he must have forgotten all about that when he left early. But I think he went home. Want me to phone and check with him?"

"Will you, honey? I was counting on that money today—I'll need some of it over the week end."

Joyce went over to the desk and sat down at it to dial Mr. Conn's number. It rang a few times and Mr. Conn's voice answered.

She'd only started to explain when he interrupted her; "Oh Lord, Joyce," he said. "I *did* forget. Will you write him a check for ninety even? And tell him I'm sorry I forgot all about it."

"All right, Mr. Conn."

She put the phone down on the hook and took the checkbook from the drawer, started to write.

Atkins called to her, "Hey, Joyce, can't you make it cash? The banks are closed by now, and tomorrow's Saturday. I don't know where I could cash it before Monday."

She looked back over her shoulder at him. "Claude, I don't know. Mr. Conn said to give you a check—Wait, I'll phone him again and ask him."

She dialed the number and got a busy signal. And it was five minutes of five now; she would have to work late on those darned handbills, and make Mr. Gutzmer wait, too. Now, whether Mr. Conn said to pay by check or told her to open the safe and pay in cash she'd never finish by five o'clock. And now that she thought of it she wasn't sure whether there was as much as ninety dollars in the cashbox anyway. There was seldom more than that and sometimes quite a bit less. She hadn't had cause to go to it or check it today. . . . Oh, of *course* there was enough money in the safe; there was that envelope with new ten dollar bills in it, at least a dozen of them. It was on the shelf where Mr. Conn kept his personal papers, insurance policies and stuff like that; but yesterday the envelope had fallen out, along with some other things, when she'd opened the safe. When she'd put it back she'd noticed what was in it.

So she could ask Mr. Conn now if it would be all right to use some of that money if there wasn't enough in the regular cash. And after all, if he'd promised to give Claude the money in cash, why would he care? Even if that money in the envelope was some he had aside for a special purpose, he could put it back any time.

She picked up the phone and dialed again, looked back

over her shoulder at Claude with humorous dismay. "Still busy," she told him.

"Say, I got an idea, Joyce. Conn probably told you to pay it by check so he'd have a record he'd paid it, see? So go ahead and write the check. Then I'll endorse it and you can cash it for me. Everybody's happy."

It was so simple an answer that she wondered why she hadn't thought of it herself. Mr. Conn couldn't possibly object to her cashing the check for Claude. It would be Mr. Conn's own check so he ought to know it wouldn't bounce. It wouldn't be like cashing somebody else's check.

"All right," she said, relieved that now she wouldn't have to keep phoning back heaven knows how many times before the line would quit being busy.

She hurried to finish writing the check and she was just giving it to Claude to endorse at the counter when the bell tinkled again and Mr. Gutzmer came in.

"Hi, Joyce," he said. "The stuff ready?"

"There are a few that aren't folded yet, Mr. Gutzmer. I'm afraid it'll take me another ten or fifteen minutes."

But he'd already seen the big pile of folded handbills on the counter and the little pile of unfolded ones beside it, and he put the piles together and picked them up. "Never mind," he told her. "I can use that many unfolded. Or fold a few myself. 'Night."

"Gee, thanks, Mr. Gutzmer. Good night."

The bell tinkled again as he went out and Joyce went over to the safe, unlocked it and opened the door. She looked in the cashbox first but she'd been right about there not being enough in it; there was somewhere around sixty dollars. But the white envelope was still there on the upper shelf and she put the cashbox back. If she had to take any of the money from the envelope she might as well take it all from the same place. She counted out nine of the crisp new tens. There seemed, she noticed, to be more of them left than she had taken, so it had been more than a dozen to begin with, probably twenty or so. She came over and counted out the nine bills again for Claude.

The check was lying there, back up, with his endorsement on it; she picked it up and started toward the safe.

He said, "Just a minute, Joyce," and she turned.

"Yes, Claude?"

"I've got to blow. I'm late now for an appointment. But I want to see you again sometime." He grinned. "How's about letting me take you for a spin in my brand new yellow convertible?"

"Why, I'd like to, Claude."

"Sunday afternoon maybe?"

"That'll be fine. But—but I don't know where to tell you to pick me up. I'm finding a new place to live tomorrow— and I don't know yet where it'll be."

"Poor little homeless girl." He pulled a pad of scratch paper toward himself on the counter and wrote a number on it. "No problem," he told her. "Here's my number. After you know where you live you can give me a ring and tell me where to pick you up. Listen, noon Sunday would be a good time to call. I'll be sure to be in then."

"All right, Claude. And—and what time—"

"Shall I pick you up? We'll decide that when you call to tell me where. High noon—I'll make a point of being there. 'Bye till then, honey."

"Good bye, Claude."

The bell tinkled again as he hurried out. She went on over to the open safe, reached for the cashbox and then changed her mind. She'd better put the endorsed check right in the envelope with the other ten dollar bills. If by any chance Mr. Conn should come in over the week end to get that money and found some of it gone, he'd wonder— unless the endorsed check was right there with the remaining bills to show him what she'd done with the missing ones. She put the check in the envelope.

A minute later, locking the front door from the outside, she saw through its glass the clock on the wall. Two minutes after five.

What a lot had happened in only twelve minutes!

His name was Darius Conn. He was forty-one years old, slender and of medium height. He had sandy hair that was perpetually mussed and often had streaks of black in it from his habit of running his fingers through it, even when his fingers were stained with printer's ink. His manner was mild and sometimes a little vague. He disliked trouble or argument. He wore shell-rimmed bifocal glasses and suffered from chronic, though usually mild, asthma.

He ran a little job printing shop on Santa Monica Boulevard in Santa Monica, California, which although it is a separate political entity is one of the hundred towns that make up the sprawling city of Los Angeles.

He paid income tax, figuring it honestly, on a net profit of a little less than five thousand dollars a year. Quite high income tax, since he was a widower and had no dependents. He looked like a man who got very little enjoyment out of life and, in most ways, he was just that kind of man.

You'd never in a thousand years have guessed that he was a murderer and a criminal. You'd have thought him dull, plodding, honest. And up to the time when, a year ago almost to the day, he had killed his wife you'd have been completely correct. Up to that time he had been a scrupulously honest man, in big and little things alike.

In little things he was still honest, from force of habit if for no other reason. But he had murdered his wife, strangled her to death with his hands, and he had got away with it. After the preliminary questioning he hadn't even been suspected; he was completely in the clear.

It had changed him.

All his life you see, he'd worked like a dog and it had got him nowhere. He'd worked as a joureyman printer and engraver for fifteen years and had saved his money. With it he'd started the little printing shop, and had found himself working harder than ever and making less money than he'd made in wages. Everything had gone wrong. The used Linotype and printing press with which he'd started had worn out within a year and had had to be replaced. Customers who owed him money went bankrupt and paid only a few cents on the dollar. A small fire only partly covered by insurance had put him farther in the red.

Through all of that and through an unhappy marriage, he'd stuck to the rules and obeyed the laws. It had been a matter of pride to him that he hadn't had even a parking ticket in eight years. Then suddenly, just like that, he was a murderer.

After the shock had worn off, after he was sure that he

was completely safe, it made him think. It made him look backward at the life behind him and realize how little he'd got out of it, and it made him look ahead into the future and to see how little hope there was for him ever to do much better unless he started making money.

A good engraver can make money.

He'd got away with murder, hadn't he? Why couldn't he get away with counterfeiting?

And why shouldn't he?

He didn't want too much out of life. A decent income without having to slave and worry for it. A chance to travel a little now and then, a change of scenery and a vacation; he hadn't been able to take a vacation worth mentioning since he'd started the shop. Decent clothes, if not expensive ones. A car that wasn't twelve years old. A woman when he wanted one.

He planned carefully. Making the plates and printing the money was only part of it.

He'd have to keep the printing shop as a front and spend some time there but he could hire a printer to take the bulk of the work off his shoulders. Maybe doing that and having time to go out and do some selling himself might even make the shop turn the corner and start to show a decent profit. But more likely it would make less, might even actually lose money for a while and for that reason he'd have to take over the bookkeeping himself, do a little finagling with it so they'd show a profit that would be reasonably consistent with the scale on which he'd be living. He wasn't going to get caught over some little detail like that. He wasn't going to get caught at all.

He started making the plates for a ten dollar bill, working slowly and carefully. At home, at night, in the little house on Stanford Street where he now lived alone. He'd kept the house instead of selling it just for that purpose. He could be sure of perfect privacy there. And he needed privacy for more than making plates and printing the bills.

Practice in disguises, for instance.

He was going to have to pass at least the first few hundred of those bills himself, to get some working capital in real money; that was going to be about the riskiest part of the deal. It would have to be done week ends at first and in various places in and around Los Angeles and the more frequently, from week end to week end, he changed his appearance, the less the risk would be.

He'd alternated between working on and practicing with those disguises and making the initial batch of ten dollar bills—three hundred of them. And the disguises were almost as good as the bills.

He had a pair of elevator shoes and and a pair of almost heelless ones. Black and brown hair dye that was easily washed out. A full theatrical make-up kit—and he'd practiced using it until he was good. He taught himself how to pad the shoulders of a coat to make himself look broad-shouldered.

He tried all of these things and others in front of a full length mirror and was sometimes surprised at what he saw there.

But the most important change a man can make in his appearance is to change the contours of his face. That's what Conn worked at hardest and with most surprising results.

He wore dentures and that's what made it easy. He'd had bad teeth in childhood and had lost so many by the time he was thirty that he'd had the rest of them pulled and had worn full dental plates for eleven years now. One set of dentures had become uncomfortable several years ago and he'd had a new set made and had kept the old ones as a spare set.

He remembered them when he was planning his disguises and had an idea that turned out to be an inspiration. He visited a dental supply bouse and bought some of the plastic material dentists use in relining or repairing plates. He went to work with it on his extra set of dentures and found he could build out the sides of them until his face became full and round, almost moonfaced. Adding a little to the front flanges changed the shape of his mouth by pushing his lips slightly forward. And thickening the roof of the upper denture changed the resonance of his voice slightly and his manner of speaking and enunciating became different.

Even without any other changes he looked like, and sounded like, a different person with those dentures in his mouth instead of his regular ones. Add the elevator shoes, shoulder padding, subtract the shell-rimmed glasses he wore ordinarily (he could see well enough for most purposes without them), blond hair dyed brown and slicked down with pomade instead of being mussed and unruly—well, he was looking at himself in that combination in the full length mirror right now and he was satisfied. He didn't think even his best friend could possibly recognize him, even in an extended conversation.

But there was no use taking chances like that. In this disguise or in any disguise he wouldn't go looking up people he knew, and he wouldn't be passing any bills in Santa Monica.

He looked at his watch and saw that it was ten minutes after five. Time to get going. Joyce had probably left the shop already, or if she hadn't she'd be gone by the time he got there.

Damn it, why hadn't he remembered to take those twenty bills away with him when he'd left the shop an hour ago? Then he wouldn't have to go back there at all. Well, it'd take him only ten minutes and it didn't really matter.

Quickly he took off the disguise and put it in the small suitcase that lay open ready for it, after this final dress rehearsal. Replaced the gimmicked dentures with his regular ones, put the trick ones in the suitcase, carefully wrapped in a towel to keep them from breaking. Put his glasses back on.

He'd left the car in front and he went out now and put the suitcase into the back seat, got behind the wheel. Good deal, he thought, that he'd made that car swap with what's-his-name? Atkins. This sedan wasn't a thing of beauty but it was a lot better mechanically than the old yellow convertible had been, and a hell of a lot less conspicuous. Worth ninety bucks difference, even though in a few months he'd probably be trading this one in on a new one. That's one thing he wasn't going to wait too long for. He'd never owned a new car in his life, and it was about time.

Not a big car nor a foreign car, nothing fancy or conspicuous, just a new car in the lower price range. A Chevrolet, a Ford or maybe a Studebaker Champion. Whichever one, most likely, would give him the best trade-in on this heap he was driving now.

He parked it around the corner from Santa Monica Boulevard on Eleventh Street and carefully locked the doors because of the suitcase in the back seat. He walked around the corner and toward the shop.

After the shop, his target for tonight—the busy district on Hollywood Boulevard around Vine Street. Plenty of shops open and doing lots of business on Friday evening.

Plan of campaign all set. Park the car on a side street, leaving all of the counterfeit tens locked in the glove compartment except one. Walk to the Hollywood-Beverly Hotel and check in. Change clothes and put on disguise in room. Walk up or down a flight or two of stairs so he wouldn't be getting on the elevator at the same floor his room was on. Take the elevator down and walk through the lobby.

At a busy drugstore buy a pack of cigarettes out of the counterfeit bill. Walk to car, stash change in glove compartment and get a second counterfeit bill. Buy something else at another store and repeat.

Each purchase would take a little time that way, but it was safer; he'd never have more than one bad bill in his possession at a time. After tonight he'd have a better idea how many bills he could pass in one evening. If it turned out to be much fewer than the twenty he'd held out (the rest of the first batch, with the plates, were in a safe deposit box at the bank), then he'd go to downtown Los Angeles tomorrow afternoon. Saturday afternoon in the downtown shopping district would surely let him get rid of the rest of the first batch.

At any rate, after this week end he'd be able to judge much better how many weeks it would take him to get rid of all of those three hundred bills. They'd bring him in a little less than three thousand of course because of his purchases in cashing them and other incidental expenses, but still net him better than two and a half thousand.

That would be all the bills he was going to risk passing in person, if he could find a wholesale outlet. There's always some risk in passing a bad bill, he knew, no matter how good the bill looks and no matter how careful you are. There's always the chance that the bartender or the cigar store clerk used to be a teller at a bank and is an expert, that he'll call copper and that the police won't accept your prepared story despite the carefully prepared, if forged, identification you have to go with it. They just might insist on holding you until they've checked thoroughly, too thoroughly, despite the fact that the bill you just tried to pass is the only one you have on you.

But that was a calculated risk he had to take. It would give him enough working capital to ease off on the number of hours he put in at the shop. And—not that he'd wait until then to start on this, of course—to make himself at home a really sizable and valuable pile of those tens. Ten thousand of them, maybe, for a face value of a hundred thousand dollars. It would probably take him six months to make that many.

Then a trip to Chicago and, under a changed identity after he got there, a leisurely and cautious look-around for an underworld connection that would let him get rid of the whole batch at one sale.

Not for face value, naturally, but his friend the police lieutenant had told him once, when it had happened to come up in casual conversation, that really good queer money sold for about thirty cents on the dollar. And his was really good, but if it brought only twenty-five cents that would give him twenty-five thousand dollars.

And that was more than he'd been able to take out of the printing shop in five years. It was worth a little risk.

His key let him in the door and he went right to the safe, turned the combination knob and pulled open the door. He put the white envelope in his inner coat pocket, closed the safe again and let himself out, walked back to the car.

After he'd unlocked the car doors and let himself in, he decided he might as well put the bills in the glove compartment of the car now instead of carrying them in his pocket. He unlocked the glove compartment, opened it, took the envelope from his pocket.

It felt lighter, he thought. He opened it and looked in.

Fewer bills, and a check. He took out the check and looked at it. Ninety dollars, Claude Atkins, *Conn's Printing Shop* rubber-stamped and Joyce Dugan's signature under it. Obverse: Claude Atkins' endorsement.

And eleven counterfeit ten dollar bills.

His first reaction was merely annoyance with Joyce. She'd made Atkins out a check as he'd told her to, but what business did she have cashing it for him? And how in hell had she known the money was there? It had been on his personal shelf in the safe, a place she had no business even looking. And he'd trusted Joyce implicitly, had even had her signature registered at the bank so she could sign routine checks, not even bothering to have her bonded since there was never more than a few hundred dollars in the account.

But she'd had no damn business *cashing* that check for Atkins; now he had only eleven bills instead of . . .

Then it hit him.

Why or how it had happened didn't matter. He was in desperate danger. Not just one but *nine* of his counterfeit bills were in the possession of a person who knew exactly where they came from. Who might take some if not all of them to his bank, who would almost certainly pass at least a few of them at places where he was known. If even one was traced back to him . . .

Sitting there behind the wheel of the car, the envelope still in his hand, Conn started sweating. Pictures flashed in his mind of a dozen ways in which Atkins might spend those bills so they could easily be traced back to him. He might pay a bill he owed with several of them. Might buy a new suit and pay for it with, say, six brand-new ten dollar bills; the clerk would remember that for sure. Might take the convertible in for a new top and pay in cash. Might (hadn't he mentioned a boarding house?) give several to his landlady, for a couple of weeks' room and board. Might (hadn't he had a folded Racing Form in his pocket?) hand one or more to a bookie—and bookies look at bills just as bank clerks do. Might, if he didn't make any major purchase over the week end, decide to put say fifty dollars of it in the bank on Monday morning. Or, if he didn't have a bank account, buy a fifty dollar bond. . . .

Useless to hope.

Possibly tomorrow, certainly no later than Tuesday, a pair of men would be calling on him at the shop or at home. "Your name is Darius Conn? We're from the Treasury Department. . . ."

And this had to happen to him before he himself had even tried to pass *one* of the bills, before he'd realized a penny of return for eleven months of careful and painstaking work, eleven months of meticulous planning. A house of cards. Now it would fall down.

How long do they sentence you for counterfeiting?

Or should he run now, while he had at least a few hours and quite possibly a few days of grace in which to get away? He could still work as a journeyman printer or Linotype operator and make a living—but it would have to be in a non-union shop because although he had an honorable withdrawal card from the International Typographical Union and could join again any time, they'd be looking for him under the name on that card. And he couldn't change it, forge a new card, because it would have to match the union's records.

And wouldn't they find him, even under another name and in a non-union shop? Knowing he was a printer . . .

And how much did he have to run with? About a hundred dollars in real money, about forty of it in his pocket and sixty in the cashbox at the shop. A couple of hundred more in the bank, but where could he cash a check for that much? Maybe in a few stores where he was known he could cash small checks, get himself a little more money. Damn it, why hadn't there been more in the damn cashbox? Then Joyce would have cashed that check out of the cashbox.

But all in all not more than a few hundred dollars, even if he counted the counterfeit. Not much to start a new life with, especially since, as he saw clearly now, he'd have to stay away from the one trade he could make a fair living at. And he had no skill aside from that trade.

But should he run?

Or did he dare risk waiting until Monday morning when his bank would be open again so he could take with him the other two hundred and eighty counterfeit tens, and the plates?

He wiped sweat off his forehead with his handkerchief.

And suddenly he was coldly calm and thinking clearly. Just as had happened—after a moment of panic like this moment of panic—after he had killed his wife.

He had to get that money back from Claude Atkins. Somehow.

No matter what the risk of doing that, it couldn't be any greater than the risk of doing nothing or the risk of running.

Get it without killing if possible, but kill if that turned out to be the only way.

He'd got away with murder once, hadn't he?

He had Atkins' address right in the glove compartment of this car that had been Atkins' car; they'd each signed over and traded registration papers.

And Atkins had had the money—he looked at his watch and saw that it was five-forty—less than an hour; it had been just before closing time that Joyce had phoned him and he'd told her to write Atkins a check.

Probably he hadn't spent any of the bills yet. Since he lived at a boarding house, quite probably he'd gone right home to clean up before eating dinner. Dinner, at a boarding house, would probably be at six, and even if Atkins was going out after dinner, it wouldn't be before six-thirty.

He had time, if he moved right away, unless Atkins lived—

Quickly he reached into the glove compartment and pulled out the car registration papers. Number 142 Worth Street, Santa Monica. For a moment he couldn't place Worth Street and then he remembered it. One of the short streets, only a block long, between Main Street and Ocean Avenue, only a block from the beach. Not over ten minutes' drive.

Plenty of time. He reached for the ignition key and then pulled his hand back. Something to decide first.

Could he go as he was, in his own identity and without a disguise, invent some story that would let him offer Atkins ninety dollars in other bills, in real bills, telling him the money the girl had given him had been—had been what? What could have been so special about those nine ten dollar bills that would be important enough that he'd be making a special trip to get them back and offer other money instead? What story could he possibly give that wouldn't make Atkins suspicious?

None that he could think of. Atkins had impressed him as a bright young man, no fool. He'd guess the score, no matter what the story. He'd guess there was something fishy—either that the money was counterfeit or that it was stolen money with known serial numbers. Likely he'd say, whether he had or not, that he'd spent *one* of the bills and trade back the other eight. Then he could—well, if he examined that one bill he held out carefully enough, comparing it with a genuine one and using a magnifying glass to check details, he could spot it. Then, if he was honest enough, he'd go to the police. If he was dishonest enough he might try blackmail, cut himself in.

Most likely he'd go to the police.

It had to be the disguise, then, and boldness. Robbery. Could he get away with it? No time to wonder that now, since he had no choice.

He started the car, U-turned and headed northeast on Santa Monica. The disguise was in the suitcase in the car, right behind him, and he could have made the change inside the printing shop, but he'd need his gun too, and that was at home. Well, he still had time.

He parked right in front of the house. No time to worry about the neighbors possibly noticing a strange man leaving his house and driving away in his car. And they'd be getting their dinners at this time of day, anyway, and not snooping out of front windows.

He made himself walk normally until he was inside the front door, and then he worked fast. Stripped off his suit and shoes, put on the suit with the heavily padded shoulders and the elevator shoes. Took off his glasses and changed his regular dentures for the gimmicked ones that made his face so different. No time to do the hair-dye job, but he'd keep his hat on. He got a felt hat from the closet; the only time Atkins had even seen him, yesterday when they'd made the car deal, he'd not been wearing a hat.

He took the revolver from the dresser drawer and put it into his coat pocket. It was a nickel-plated thirty-two, a small gun. He'd bought it a few weeks after he was married; Myrtle had insisted on his buying one when she'd learned how often he had to go back to the shop after dinner and work late there, sometimes until after midnight, leaving her home alone. He hadn't wanted to get the gun; he'd tried to talk her in to getting a good dog instead, but Myrtle hadn't liked dogs.

The gun had never been fired. He'd never thought of it when he'd killed Myrtle.

A quarter after six when he left the house, not quite half past when he got to Worth Street. Parked half a block away because the car had, until yesterday evening, been Atkins' car and anyone at the boarding house might recognize it if he parked it right in front. But one dark blue sedan is like another at half a block's distance.

The old yellow convertible wasn't in sight. He hoped that meant Atkins had put it away for the night wherever he kept a car and didn't intend to go out.

He made himself sit there in the car for a minute or two, calming himself down, and running over in his mind the plan he'd worked out, the exact wording of his approach—an approach and a plan that he'd have to be able to vary according to circumstances but which had to have a starting point. "Mr. Atkins? I'm Herbert Barry, an attorney. There's a matter I'd like to discuss with you, a matter that is in your own interest—in fact, something considerably to your advantage. But there's an angle to it that's rather private and personal. I wonder if we could—uh—go to your room a moment to discuss it?"

Curiosity and avarice, the suggestion of gain. That ought to do it. "Why, sure," Atkins would say.

In the room: the gun, holdup, get wallet, make Atkins face the other way and slug him on the back of the head with the barrel of the gun. So he'd fall across the bed, if possible. Try to catch him and ease him down otherwise. Hit a second time to kill if there was even the faintest suspicion that Atkins might have recognized him through the disguise. Get out of there, fast, before anyone stopped him.

Crude, yes. But it's bold and crude crimes that work, not fancy ones. He'd learned that when he'd killed his wife.

And what's a second murder when you've done one? Better, he told himself, to take one big chance now and get it over with than to spend the rest of his life—or as much of it as mattered—in jail or in hiding.

He got out of the car, walked to the house and up onto the porch. Rang the bell.

A woman came to the door and opened it. A gaunt, severe woman with gray hair and bright, bird-like eyes, wearing an apron over a faded dress. "Yes?" she asked.

"Is Mr. Claude Atkins home?"

"No. Didn't eat here tonight."

"Oh. Do you know when he'll be back?"

She shook her head, started to close the door. He said quickly, "I'm sorry, but it's desperately important that I find him right away. Do you know where he went?"

She looked at him hesitantly a moment, and he said, "It's

really very important. To him. I'll promise he won't mind your telling me."

"Well—it's his girl's birthday. He's having dinner with her, at her place. Her name's Harper, Rose Harper, and she's got an apartment over on Pico but I don't know the address."

"Would anyone else here know? The address I mean."

She shook her head. "No, but you might get it outa the phone book. She's got a phone, because he calls her all the time."

"May I use your phone book?"

She moved aside not too willingly to let him in. "Over there," she said. The phone was a pay phone on the wall; on a table nearby lay Western and Central directories.

He opened the Western one, fumbled through to the H's, found a column of Harpers, ran his finger down—Ralph C., Richard, Richard J., Robert B., Robert R.—Rose, 1590 Pico.

He closed the book and started back toward the door.

"Thanks," he said, "thanks an awful lot." And he meant it.

Back to the car. Luckily it was parked facing so he wouldn't have to drive it past the house. He might have aroused her curiosity to the extent that she'd be watching out and might recognize the car if it went right past her.

Main Street to Pico and east on Pico, watching the numbers as soon as he'd crossed Lincoln. He was still in the 1400 block when he saw the yellow convertible he'd traded Atkins. It was parked facing south in front of Woodlawn Cemetery. He drove past slowly looking, on the other side of the street from the parked car, for 1590. It was right across from a hardware store, he saw when he got near enough and when he was in front of the store he saw a door alongside it with 1590 lettered over it.

He drove on past. In the middle of the next block he U-turned and parked half a block behind the convertible, facing the same way.

Sat there, thinking. He'd found Claude Atkins. The convertible proved it. But what now?

Go upstairs, get in on a pretext, and try to shoot both of them? Too risky. There must be other apartments up there, for one thing, people who'd hear shots. The building had only two stories, but it was quite deep and no doubt the second story had at least four apartments up there, especially if they were small ones such as a girl alone would live in. Or, come to think, how did he know she lived alone? She might be rooming with another girl and that might mean there could be three of them up there. Too risky, if there was a better way, a safer way.

Besides, he didn't like the idea of killing a girl if he didn't have to.

Much better, much safer, if he could get Atkins alone, make it look like a simple holdup.

But what if, after dinner at the girl's place, they both went out? It was her birthday and quite probably they'd go somewhere to celebrate, especially since she was providing the eats. And especially with ninety dollars cash burning a hole in Atkins' pocket.

He looked at his watch. Was there time—? Good, God, it was only six-fifty. Not much more than an hour since he'd discovered that Atkins had got those nine bills. He had plenty of time. If they were going out after a birthday dinner at the girl's place, surely they wouldn't be leaving before half past seven, and eight would be more likely.

He had at least half an hour. If there was a phone nearby—

He got out of the car and looked around both ways. Yes, there was a tavern sign in the next block west. A restaurant, rather, but there was a smaller sign under the restaurant sign that read *Cocktails,* so it had a bar attached. And he could use a drink, along with the phone call.

He hurried there as fast as he could walk.

The bar was dimly lighted as are all Los Angeles cocktail bars. A woman and two men sat at the other end of it; aside from them and a bartender polishing glasses, the place was empty. Conn didn't see a telephone but of course there'd be one.

He fished the change out of his pocket to make sure he had dimes for the phone call. There were only pennies and a half a dollar.

He put the half dollar on the bar as the bartender came toward him. "Can I have dimes for that? I want a bourbon and soda but I want to make a call while you get it."

"Sure," the bartender said. He went to the register with the half dollar and came back with five dimes. "Bonded bourbon?"

"Yeah. Where's the phone?"

The bartender jerked a finger toward the passageway that led to the restaurant.

The phone was in a cubicle recessed into the wall of the passage. There wasn't any door to the cubicle, but no one was within earshot anyway so that didn't matter. He had to stop and look up the listing again. He'd memorized the address but hadn't looked at the phone number. For a frantic moment he couldn't remember the girl's name, then he had it, Rose Harper.

He found the number, dropped a dime and dialed it.

"Hello." It was a girl's voice, a nice voice. He hoped he wouldn't have to kill her.

He made his own voice businesslike. "This is Pico 4-8223, Rose Harper?"

"Yes, speaking."

"This is the General Telephone Company, repair department. Has your phone been in use or off the hook in the last ten minutes?"

"Why—no, it hasn't."

"And it hasn't rung?"

"No, it hasn't."

"We had a complaint from a party who tried to reach you and couldn't. I tried four times myself in the last ten minutes and this is the first time your phone rang, you're sure?"

"Of course I'm sure. I've been right here."

"Circuits here are all right. It must be something in your phone box. May we send a man to check it?"

"Certainly."

"You'll be home all evening?"

"Yes, I'll be home."

"Thank you." He hung up quickly before she might ask any questions.

Leisurely now, because there was no hurry, he went back to the bar and to the drink that was waiting for him.

They weren't going out after dinner, and that made it a lot easier and a lot better. Now he was no longer faced with the risk of going up there and doing the job when there were at least two of them in the girl's apartment, nor the risk of their going out for the evening and spending some of that money in ways in which it might be traced back to them.

Now it was only a matter of getting Atkins alone after he left, and surely he wouldn't be leaving before ten o'clock, maybe much later. He could even go back and wait for him at the rooming house. But what if he went in the back way, from a garage somewhere in the alley behind the house? If only he knew where Atkins put the car at night, that would be the perfect place to wait for him, hidden in a dark garage. But there was no way he could find that out now.

The hallway and stairway that led up to the apartment over the hardware store? Possible. He'd look it over.

But first this drink. Just one because his head had to be clear. He sipped it slowly, enjoying it.

He'd improvise, somehow. Improvisation, being ready to take a chance when the chance came, that was the trick. That was how he'd got away with killing his wife. He hadn't planned it at all, it had happened suddenly, but then he had improvised.

He found himself thinking about Myrtle. About what a bitch she'd been, about how stupid he'd been not to have realized sooner what a fool she'd been making of him. But in the end she'd been the one who'd been stupid. He'd never have killed her if only she'd left bad enough alone that night, if only she hadn't goaded him to desperation that way. He'd never have found out, then, that he was a man after all and not a mouse. And that murder was a simple thing.

At least Myrtle had taught him that.

But she'd given him three years of hell first. Murdering her hadn't been a mistake; marrying her had.

A mistake down the line. She'd been ten years younger than he for one thing; he'd been thirty-seven then, four years ago, and she'd been twenty-seven. But that age difference had been less important than the difference in their tastes. Myrtle had wanted always to go out, to be taken dancing, drinking, to shows, anywhere. He'd wanted mostly quiet evenings at home—the few evenings he didn't have to go back to the shop to work late—quiet evenings to rest up from hard work, damned hard work.

And the lack of money had been even more important than that difference between them. Myrtle was extravagant, or wanted to be. He'd made a big mistake in not telling her, before they were married, just how little money he could draw from the shop every week without bankrupting himself. She'd probably assumed it to be three or four times as much and unfortunately she'd never asked him; if she had he wouldn't have lied to her and that would have no doubt ended things between them then and there, before they'd taken the irrevocable step of getting married. Irrevocable because Myrtle didn't believe in divorce.

God, that first night home after their brief honeymoon—he'd saved up months for *that*—when she'd complained about the size of the little house on Stanford Street and had demanded a bigger and better one. And he'd had to explain to her that, besides a very small equity in the house, every penny he had was tied up in the business and that he couldn't possibly take out of the business more than seventy or eighty dollars a week, just then or in the near future. But that someday—

Myrtle wasn't interested in someday. From then on she was alternately sullen and nagging. Only occasionally was she pleasant to him. Most of the time, nearly all of the time, she slept alone to punish him for real or imaginary offenses, however slight, in the time-honored tradition of wives who enjoy hurting their husbands in every possible way.

And hurt it did, because the hell of it was that he still wanted her. Wanted her body, anyway. It had been *that*, not the fact that he'd caught her in adultery, that had been the topper. If only, besides taunting him, she hadn't flaunted her body at him that night . . .

It had been a Friday night, the first Friday in February. He didn't remember the exact date any more but it was the first Friday because it had been his lodge night. The one night a month he went out alone, except the nights when he went back to the shop. Myrtle had talked him into joining a lodge, two years before. She'd have been pleased to see him join several of them, even though it would cut down the number of evenings she could nag him to take her places. Myrtle's father had been a strong lodge man, a joiner, and had impressed on his family the advantages to a businessman of membership in fraternal organizations. Myrtle had the idea that the more friends he made among other Santa Monica businessmen the more orders he'd get and the more money he'd make. He'd never been able to see that it made any difference; his lodge brothers gave him business only when he underbid the competition. And it was the low prices forced by competition that kept him from making more money, not lack of enough work to keep him busy.

But that night he'd gone—or had started to go. Halfway to the lodge hall he'd decided the hell with it. He was feeling lower than usual that night and felt that some drinks would do him more good. He'd never been much of a drinker, especially since his marriage had so sharply limited his pocket money, but that night he felt that a bit of drinking would do him more good than harm. And, for once, he had a little more money than Myrtle knew he had.

Or had that been his real reason? At the back of his mind had been a certain tavern on Second Street in which a few times, years ago, before he'd met Myrtle, he'd picked up women. Probably the place had changed; there'd been that reform wave and clean-up. There was probably a pretty slim chance of his finding an unattached woman there tonight and being able to pick her up, but—It had been a long time since his wife had deigned to give the privilege of her body. Weeks at least.

Anyway, he'd gone to the tavern. It *had* changed and it offered him nothing in the way of unattached women.

But, as things turned out, it offered him something vastly more important; it offered him an ironclad alibi for murder that had not yet been committed. It offered him Henry Jennings.

Jennings was head teller in the bank Conn used and was, as all tellers must be to gain and hold their jobs, a man of unimpeachable character.

But even men of unimpeachable character occasionally escape from their wives and the conventions to get out for an evening's drinking, and this was such an evening for Jennings. He was well started when Conn came into the tavern, and he was lonesome and eager for someone to talk to. Not being a practiced *bon vivant*, and not knowing anyone in the moderately crowded tavern, he had not known how to go about getting into conversation with strangers, so he'd hailed Conn like a long lost brother even though they'd known one another but slightly.

Drinks had been bought back and forth and a couple of hours later Conn was feeling cheerful instead of depressed and had completely given up the idea of looking for a woman. In fact, he had just decided to go home early to Myrtle—it was ten o'clock then—in the belief that tonight she would change her mind and give herself to him. He'd much rather have had Myrtle than the hypothetical other woman anyway.

But he had difficulty in prying himself away from Jennings and finally, to avoid argument, he had used the subterfuge of heading for the can and going out the back way. He drove straight home, a little faster than he would have driven ordinarily.

He sobered immediately when the first thing he saw on entering the door was a man's raincoat hanging on the hat-rack in the hallway. It wasn't his and it hadn't been there when he'd left at seven.

With sudden fury in his heart—not against Myrtle as yet but against the other man—he ran into the bedroom. But Myrtle was in bed alone, reading a love story magazine and eating chocolates. He looked quickly in the closet and under the bed, even ran out into the kitchen and tooked there.

The man had left. Conn went back to the bedroom and stared at his wife. From the way her hair and make-up were mussed, he knew that the man had just left, only minutes ago. And Myrtle was naked under the sheet. Her bare shoulders proved that.

What he might have said to her, he'd never know, for he didn't have a chance to speak, never said a word.

Myrtle started talking first, and she defied him. She told him sure there'd been a man there and it wasn't any of his damned business he wasn't a man himself and what was he going to do about it?

Even then nothing much might have happened, even then he might never have laid a hand on her.

But she made the mistake of getting out of bed. She got up and stood there to revile him, arms akimbo, stark naked.

And her body, at thirty, was still beautiful, still what he wanted and all he wanted. And another man only minutes ago had had his pleasure of it and Conn knew that he would never have her again, no matter what happened now.

For the first time in his life he had completely lost his head. He stepped forward and hit her a blow with his fist that knocked her unconscious back across the bed, and then his hands were around her throat choking; they didn't let go until she was dead.

Then suddenly all emotion was gone. He was calm.

He sat down quietly to decide what he was going to do and at first it was a simple choice between calling the police and killing himself. There were sleeping capsules in the medicine cabinet that would have done the job easily and painlessly.

Suddenly it occurred to him that there was a chance, a slim chance, that he wouldn't have to do either of those things. He didn't expect it to work because he'd never been lucky; all the breaks had always gone against him. But he had nothing to lose.

If the bank teller was still at the tavern on Second Street and didn't realize how long Conn had been gone—

It was an outside chance but he took it because he wanted to live. He took the chance without much hope, but he took it.

It had taken him less than ten minutes to drive home from the tavern and after that things had happened so fast that not over another ten had elapsed. Luckily he'd left his car in front of the house instead of putting it in the garage. The garage was difficult to drive into from the alley, especially at night, and he always left the car in front when he'd been drinking to any extent.

He drove back to the tavern and went in by the back door. It was as he had left it, still moderately crowded, and Jennings was still alone at the bar staring moodily now at his reflection in the blue glass of the backbar mirror. Conn's own glass, still with part of a drink in it, still stood there beside Jennings; if the bartender had tried to take it away Jennings must have told him not to.

Conn stepped up to his glass at the bar. He remembered what they'd been talking about and picked up the conversation right where they'd left it.

Jennings was still in a mood to talk, but he was getting a bit fuzzy to make too much sense. Still, he didn't seem on the verge of a blackout, so Conn decided to hold onto him as long as it seemed safe. But he nursed his own drinks and unobtrusively slowed Jennings down too. He pretended to be hungry and ordered some cold pickled frankfurters from the backbar, and some potato chips. He got Jennings to eat too.

He managed to keep the status quo until midnight and then, carefully pointing out that it was midnight, suggested they'd better knock it off, but managed to stretch things another half hour and sober Jennings up a little more by suggesting they stop in the restaurant around the corner for some coffee before they drove home.

He got home the second time at twelve-forty, and he phoned the police at once.

He was icily calm—the police had thought he was in a state of shock—throughout the questioning that had followed.

His story was simple and the police couldn't shake it. He'd left home around seven, had driven part way to the lodge hall and had then changed his mind and had driven to the tavern on Second Street. He'd run into Jennings there at not later than seven-thirty, and they'd been together at the tavern until midnight. Then they'd spent about half an hour at the restaurant and separated. He'd returned home, found his wife dead, and had phoned the police.

There wasn't a thing to disprove his story and plenty to confirm it. Jennings, roused from sleep after they had finally learned his home address at three in the morning, confirmed it. He'd been with Conn, he said, from before eight o'clock until after midnight and neither of them had been out of the other's sight for longer than a few minutes at a time—five minutes at the outside—when one or the other of them had gone to the john at the tavern.

And the medical examiner put the time of Myrtle's death at not before nine-thirty or after ten-thirty.

Besides, there was ample indication that Myrtle Conn had entertained, and entertained well, another man than her husband. Besides the raincoat, which didn't fit Conn, there were other indications that another man had been there. There were two glasses—Conn hadn't noticed them—from which whisky had been drunk. One contained Myrtle's fingerprints, the other fingerprints that were too blurred for positive identification but which definitely weren't Conn's. Cigarette butts in the bedroom ash tray were of a brand that neither Conn nor his wife smoked.

Long before the gray dawn the police were thoroughly convinced that Conn was innocent and that Myrtle's lover had, for whatever reason, killed her.

The next day the police found the clincher. Canvassing the neighborhood, they found the inevitable snoopy neighbor who had seen a man wearing a raincoat enter the Conn house at about half past eight. From the distance of her house, across the street and three doors away, she couldn't describe the man but she was sure it wasn't Conn. She'd been curious, she admitted, because she'd known the Conns slightly but well enough to know that this was Conn's lodge night. So she'd watched the house off and on until she'd seen the man leaving, without his raincoat, a little before ten o'clock.

Naturally she'd quit watching then, so she hadn't seen Conn drive up a few minutes later. Nobody had seen him.

The bartender at the tavern on Second Street and those of the customers whom the police were able to locate weren't able to confirm the alibi which Jennings had given Conn but neither were they able to deny it. He'd been there all right, but they couldn't affirm as Jennings did that he'd been there all the time; however, none of them had seen him leave or return.

It had been that simple.

It hadn't hurt Conn's case either, especially the first night before the evidence that cleared him mounted, that a friend of his, Charlie Barrett, was a sergeant of detectives and was on duty at the Santa Monica station when the case had broken. He hadn't been assigned to it, but the good word he'd put in for Conn had eased the situation and had probably held off the third-degree type of questioning that might possibly have broken him during those first horrible hours before he knew whether Jennings would or would not remember that half hour's absence of his from the tavern and before he knew whether or not any of his neighbors on Stanford Street had seen him come home and leave again, or had seen his car parked in front during those ten minutes he'd been inside.

So the investigation had concentrated on an attempt to learn the identity of Myrtle's visitor and presumed murderer. Conn, quite genuinely, hadn't been able to help them in the slightest. There was no reason to suspect any of his friends; no doubt it had been someone Myrtle had met and had been meeting the times she'd gone out alone—always presumably to a movie—nights he'd been working late or had been too tired to go out with her.

Within a week, when it was obvious that the investigation was getting no farther down the blind alley into which it had been diverted, Darius Conn had known for certain that he had got away with murder.

And without regret. Myrtle had had it coming, had deserved it. But, quite illogically . . . he missed her. No woman would ever again be to him what Myrtle had been, between the time he'd first met her and the end of their honeymoon. Or even in the three years of their marriage after the honeymoon, the infrequent times he'd been able to rouse her to passion. No woman's body would ever be to him what hers had been.

Yes, when he'd killed her, when he'd *had* to kill her, something in himself had died too.

Yes, he still missed her.

He was missing her now, making wet circles on the smooth black plastic of the bar top. With a glass that was now empty.

He looked at his watch again. No hurry, it was only a little after seven. But he shouldn't have another.

Outside, it was just getting dark. The old yellow convertible was still there so all was well.

He didn't cross the street to his own car; he walked toward the hardware store instead. Now would be a good time to look over the setup there, particularly the hallway.

There was a light on in the hallway now. Through the curtain over the glass in the upper half of the door you could see in from the outside, but not very clearly.

He opened the door and went inside. The hallway itself was wider than the width of the doorway. It was about seven feet wide. The stairway, along the outside of the building, started a few feet from the door, a passageway led alongside and back past them.

Six mailboxes along the passageway. The apartments were quite small then, not over two rooms apiece if there were six of them. He moved to the mailboxes. No. 1, L. Davis. No. 2, Franken. No. 3, Rose Harper.

She did live alone then, not with a family or a roommate.

There were just two of them up there. Atkins and the girl.
He could . . . No, it was too dangerous. If the girl screamed
or if he had to use the gun, up to five other hallway doors
could burst open before he could get away. *Someone* would
have the nerve to follow him out into the street even
if no one had the nerve to try to follow him farther. But
they'd see him get in the car, get the license number when
he drove past or even when he U-turned, if he did it that
way. . . . Or he could take Atkins' keys too, make his getaway in the convertible—no, the police cars would have a
flash on it in minutes, and he'd never have a chance in a
car as conspicuous as that. And if he made his getaway
in his victim's car, the police, if they were smart, would
take the license numbers of all other cars parked nearby and
when they checked the blue sedan and found it had been
Atkins' car until last night that would be it.

He went back along the passage. There was a door that
must lead to a broom closet, under the stairway. He tried
the knob and found it locked. But the shape of the keyhole
showed that it should open with an ordinary skeleton key
and he had one of that type on his key ring, the key to the
back door of his house. (He'd have replaced that lock with a
Yale lock long before except there was a good strong bolt on
the inside of the back door; he kept it bolted and came and
went by the front door, or by the side door if he was going
to or coming from the garage. In fact, there was no real reason for him to have kept that key on his ring, but he was
glad now that he had.)

It opened the broom closet door. The closet held a mop
and broom, a mop bucket and a few other things but there
was still plenty of room in it.

Perfect, for his ambush. He could stay in that closet and
he'd hear anybody coming down the stairs. If a man's footsteps, he could be in time to intercept right at the foot of the
stairs and—if it wasn't Atkins, of course, he'd have to pretend to be leaving the building and come back in a few minutes later. But there wouldn't be a lot of traffic on those
stairs after dark.

To try it for size, and for hearing, he stepped into the closet
and pulled the door shut behind him. Silence, for what
seemed to be ten or fifteen minutes. Then he heard a door
open and close upstairs, footsteps—a woman's footsteps,

click of high heels. She took about fifteen steps before she reached the stairs; he could tell the difference in the sound immediately when she started down them.

He waited until the outer door had closed behind her and then came out of the closet. He looked at his watch and frowned when he saw that his wait had been less than five minutes. It had seemed much longer. He was going to have a hell of a long wait in there if Atkins stayed late.

But he'd learned something important. He'd been able to hear footsteps in the hallway upstairs before the girl or woman had reached the stairs. He could have counted them. If he knew just how far from the stairs the door of the Harper girl's apartment was, he wouldn't have to leave his hiding place if he heard footsteps that reached the stairs too soon or took too long to reach them.

He closed the closet door again but left it unlocked, went back to the front and walked up the stairs. He didn't have to go any further than the head of them; the door right across was numbered *three*.

That would make it really easy. Only two steps to the stairs; if there were more than that, it wouldn't be Atkins.

He went down the stairs again, outside and across the street to his car. No use waiting in the closet yet. Surely, since they were spending the evening there, Atkins wouldn't be leaving until nine at the very earliest. Ten-thirty or eleven would be more likely, quite possible even later, especially since tomorrow was Saturday.

He'd probably have a damned long wait in that closet if he started his vigil at nine and there was certainly no use starting it now, at half past seven. Meanwhile, he'd watch the door from his car and if Atkins did leave early for any reason he'd have to follow the convertible and change his plans, improvise again.

He made sure no one was coming along the sidewalk and then took the revolver out of his pocket to check it. Despite the fact that he'd already done so when he'd taken it from the drawer at home, he broke out the cylinder and spun it, checking that it was fully loaded. Clicked the cylinder back and made sure it locked in position.

Small gun though it was, it felt satisfyingly heavy in his hand. Swung hard, it would make an excellent bludgeon. He hoped he'd be able to use it that way and not have to take the risk of firing it. And Atkins hadn't been wearing a hat last night so he probably wouldn't be wearing one tonight.

That red hair would make a fine target. Probably the best plan would be to come out of the closet while Atkins was coming down the stairs, set a pace to reach the door just behind him. Strike from behind as he reached to open the door. Grab the wallet and get out quickly.

He put the gun back in his pocket and sat quietly, watching the doorway. He felt perfectly calm now, completely confident.

His name was Claude Atkins and he was a very frightened young man, although he was trying his best not to show it and felt pretty sure he was succeeding. At least Rose hadn't seemed to notice it. Very confident Rose seemed tonight, serenely confident. Despite the fact that he loved her, or felt pretty sure that he loved her, he found himself resenting that confidence just a bit—but his resentment was nothing compared to his fright.

Five days now he'd been frightened, ever since last Sunday evening when he'd suddenly found himself proposing marriage to Rose Harper—and having the proposition accepted. Worse, finding himself discussing the date and finding that it was being set for the second of June less than four months off. Finding plans being made, damnably definite plans.

They'd each arrange to get a week off or take a week off the first week in June and they'd spend their honeymoon in Ensenada, Mexico. Rose had been in California only a year and a half and she'd never got as far south as Mexico, not even to one of the border towns. And the border towns weren't really *Mexico* anyway, but she'd heard that Ensenada, only a little over a hundred miles in, was really wonderful, and it would be an easy day's drive each way and not an expensive trip like going to Mexico City would be; they'd have to fly to get there and back and flying cost a lot.

But the second of June, they found after checking a little calendar card Claude kept in his wallet, was a Saturday and that would be the best day. They could get married

Saturday morning and be in Ensenada by late afternoon or early evening; if they drove back the following Sunday that would give them a full week there, a little longer than a week really.

And Rose would keep on working for at least a few more months and maybe as long as a year until they had some nice furniture and had it paid for. She had a little over two hundred dollars saved up in the bank and they could use that as a down payment on furniture. (She'd been a bit surprised to learn that he didn't have *anything* saved up, but she'd taken it in her stride.) And both of them working for a while would get them off to a good start and—

And there it was and he was hooked. No way out of it now except by hurting Rose and he wouldn't do that for a million dollars because she was a swell girl and damn it, he *did* love her, and if he had to get married at all Rose was sure the girl he'd pick but—

The only trouble is that he didn't really want to get married at all. He didn't want to give up all the things that marriage would make him give up—and give up permanently. Once you're in, once you have kids especially (and somehow he knew without having specifically asked that Rose wanted children) it's too late to change your mind and back out.

And it would change everything. Right now, although he wasn't ahead of the game, he had everything he really wanted except Rose. Now he was going to have Rose, but it meant giving up just about everything else, including and especially his way of life. He couldn't be carefree any more, quit a job whenever he felt like it, take some time off and have fun before he looked for another.

By trade he was garage mechanic, and he made anywhere from fifty to seventy-five dollars a week, take-home pay, and it was plenty. For him. It got him everything important that he wanted, and he hadn't had a serious worry in the world—until last Sunday evening. But how far was it going to go in supporting two people, and maybe eventually God knows how many people?

He knew plenty of married men who were making about the same money he usually made. They had to carry their lunches. They had to go home from the tavern after one or two drinks because that was all their pocket money would let them have—and besides the little woman was waiting home and she'd raise hell if they were late. They had to scheme and scrimp for a year before they could buy a new set of golf clubs or a new camera or something. If they got into poker games they had to quit when they'd lost the few bucks they had. If they bet the ponies it had to be fifty cent bets that their wives didn't know about. And weekends and any other time off they had they'd be mowing the lawn, painting the floor, or some damn thing.

All that he was letting himself in for, and for the rest of his life. And why?

Because he wanted to sleep with Rose and hadn't been able to, that's why. Well, that wasn't all of it. He'd come to like her a lot in the four months he'd known her, to feel an increasing feeling of *something* toward her that he presumed was love. A kind of tenderness. A protective feeling. A big kick out of kissing her, out of touching her, however casually.

But that was another thing, another damned worry. Even now that they were engaged, she still wouldn't let him really touch her. Not pet her, that is. Kiss her, yes, put his arms around her, that sort of thing. But not touch her breasts, for instance, even for God's sake outside her dress.

He'd thought being engaged to her, having asked her to marry him (and finding the date so definite and so unexpectedly soon) would have changed *that*.

But it hadn't, and it worried him that it hadn't. What if she was frigid? He'd read books; he knew there were women who were frigid and never really enjoyed sex. He didn't think Rose was that way, judging from the way she kissed him sometimes, but how did he *know*? For that matter, if she was still a virgin—and he believed she was or why *wouldn't* she, now that they were going to be married—how did she herself know what the score was? Maybe she'd find she didn't like it, and then where would they be? Especially if she wasn't sure at first, or pretended because she loved him, and let things go along but with sex relations between them getting less and less frequent until they'd had a couple of kids, and then the mess he'd be in. Jesus. He'd heard guys talk about it. One poor sucker—he was thirty-five but a guy that old must still want it even if not as often—had told him he hadn't slept with his wife for three years, but because they had four kids and he loved the kids and didn't make enough to do anything about it, there wasn't anything he *could* do about it.

Of course he appreciated a girl being good, and one of the reasons he'd liked Rose so much was that she was a good girl, but there was that awful chance you took. On top of everything else. You gave up everything else, your freedom and your spending money and tied yourself down to the straight and narrow and no horsing around (because you couldn't afford it, if for no other reason), all because you wanted a woman of your own to sleep with every night, and then if you weren't (what was the word?) compatible, you were stuck just the same. A hell of a mess marriage *could* be, unless you had a lot of money. Which he didn't. Or unless you were enough of a son-of-a-bitch just to walk out. Which he wasn't. He wasn't even son-of-a-bitch enough to break an engagement.

And right now, sitting back comfortably in an overstuffed chair, watching Rose wash dishes in the little kitchenette (He'd offered to help but she wouldn't let him.), he didn't want to break it.

Rose was beautiful. Not just pretty like most of the girls he knew, but really beautiful. Beautiful like movie stars are beautiful. He should quit worrying, he thought, and realize how lucky he was. With a girl like Rose in love with him—

And she must really love him, he thought; she sure wasn't marrying him for his money or even for security. She could easily get a guy who made more money and had better prospects than a grease monkey. And a pretty unambitious grease monkey at that, he had to admit.

Damn it, maybe this was the best thing that could have happened to him. He was twenty-five, wasn't he? About time he cut down on helling around and changing jobs and working only when he felt like it. He could get a job in a good big garage where there was a chance to work up to service manager or something, get some money saved up and maybe start a small place of his own, or a partnership if he could find the right guy, build up a business, get somewhere. Maybe meanwhile, on the side, make some money by buying up old heaps, one or two at a time, fixing them up to look good and run sweet and selling them for twice what he'd paid for them.

He could start with what he had, the convertible he'd swapped the printer for. Some new canvas, a couple of week ends of work; he could get four hundred for it, maybe even five. It was old, but basically it was a damn good car. With ninety bucks difference he'd sure got the best of the bargain on it.

Rose was taking off her apron now. She came over and sat down on the arm of the overstuffed chair, and he put his arm around her.

"Hi," he said.

"Hi yourself, Redhead. Claude, how come you aren't called Red?"

"Had a brother who had lots redder hair than mine. So he got called Red. I didn't rate."

"*Had* a brother? Is he—?"

"Yeah. Killed in an auto accident four years ago. He was three years older than I was. I was twenty-one when he was killed; he was twenty-four. I guess that happening the way it did and when it did kind of helped make me—well, helped make me like I am."

"How do you mean, Claude?"

"Not much good. Not very ambitious, not able to settle down to one thing or one job, save money and get somewhere. Only I know I got to change now, if we're getting married."

"If? Aren't you sure, Claude?"

Something in her voice brought back all the tenderness he'd felt last Sunday night. He pulled her gently but firmly off the chair arm and down into his lap. "Didn't mean it that way, honey. I'm crazy about you."

She put her head on his shoulder. "Tell me more about your brother. What you meant by saying his being killed did something to you."

"Well—I was crazy about him. He was a wonderful guy, Rose. And he was ambitious as hell and worked hard and saved his dough, was going to have a business of his own and make good. Didn't hell around, didn't drink except maybe a beer once in a while, worked or studied evenings instead of having dates—studied television servicing, that's what he was going in for. And he got a shop of his own when he was only twenty-three, two years younger than I am now—and lost his shirt, everything he'd saved. Even went in debt before he had to give it up. Had to go back to work for somebody else and paying off and it'd have taken him two-three years to do that before he could even think of starting something for himself again.

"And then he got killed. Not his own fault. Driving back to the TV store he worked for after making a delivery, early one evening. On Olympic. A drunk bats out of a side street past a stop sign smack into him. He didn't have a chance."

Rose's hand on his arm tightened. "I'm sorry, Claude. That was awful."

"Damn right it was awful. Good thing the other guy got killed too or I'd have done it myself. Well, anyway, ever since then I've thought about all the work Red did, all the things he gave up, all the fun he missed, and—well, it made breaking my neck to get anywhere seem kind of foolish. You understand what I mean, honey?"

"Sure, but—"

"Yeah, I know. I got to change now. So I will. That kind of stuff is all right if you're single and going to stay single, but not if you want to get married."

"Claude, are you *sure* you want to get married?"

"I'm sure I want to marry *you*. Anyway, it's about time I straightened up a little, or I might end up down on Skid Row, if I lived that long. Listen Rose, I'm going to get you an engagement ring tomorrow. Want to help pick it out? I wouldn't even know the size or anything."

"I thought you said you didn't have any money saved. I don't want you to buy one on time. I'd rather you started saving."

"Honey, you ought to have *some* kind of an engagement ring. And if it's not an expensive one, I can buy it for cash. Or not owe much on it. I didn't tell you yet, but I swapped cars with a guy last night."

"Swapped cars?"

"Yeah, and got ninety bucks difference. The old blue sedan for an old yellow convertible. I put some work on it and maybe twenty-five, thirty dollars for parts and stuff and it'll be at least as good as the one I had and I'll be ahead on the deal. Enough to buy a ring or almost enough."

"Honestly, Claude, I'd rather not have one. Especially since it's only going to be a few months."

"Not even to show off to the other girls at the restaurant?"

"No, I'm not even going to tell them. I don't care much for any of them, and you know I hate that job. I want to get back to bookkeeping so I'll have more regular hours, the same ones you work, especially after we're married."

"Okay, honey, if you really don't want one."

"I don't. Instead, you start your saving with that money. With fifty dollars of it anyway, since you'll need some to fix up that car. You go right down and open up a bank account tomorrow."

"Monday. Tomorrow's Saturday. Sure, Rose. Only listen, I might do something foolish with it over the week end. Especially with you working both tomorrow and Sunday so you can't keep me out of trouble."

"Claude, haven't you got enough responsibility—"

He laughed. "Give me time. I just put in an order for some but maybe it hasn't been delivered yet. You keep that fifty for me. Hey, you've got a bank account. Why don't you just put it in there Monday so I won't have to open one?"

"Well—I suppose I could but—but only if you'll let me give you a receipt for it."

"Okay. Look, there's no sense in my starting an account just for a few months, is there? Just put it in yours and we'll start a joint account after we're married."

"If you'll give me something every week out of your pay, all right, I'll hold it for us. But I'm going to give you a receipt each time so you'll know just how much it is in case—"

He chuckled. "There isn't going to be any 'in case,' baby. But if you want to do it that way, I suppose it's your training as a bookkeeper. Listen, that bottle of wine I brought. It'll be cold by—"

The phone rang.

Rose untangled herself and went to answer it. She said, "Yes," a couple of times and then, "All right, Mr. Howard. I'll be there." She put back the receiver.

"The boss," she told Claude. "Two of the girls on the early shift are sick and he wants me to start at five instead of at eleven."

"Five? You mean five o'clock in the *morning*?"

She smiled at him. "Don't sound so horrified, darling. Don't you see what that means? I'll be through working early in the afternoon, at half-past one. And haven't you been complaining for weeks now because I could never get a

Saturday afternoon or a Sunday afternoon off so we could take a drive somewhere? Well, tomorrow's Saturday. Or do you have other plans already?"

His face had brightened. "No. Gee, that's swell. Sure, I'll spend tomorrow morning working on the car to get it fixed up—I'll get it cleaned up anyway. And pick you up right at the restaurant at one-thirty?"

She nodded. "But you'll have to leave awfully early tonight. I'll have to be in bed by nine to get up at four. And I want to bathe and—" She looked at the clock. "It's almost eight. I'm afraid you'd better not stay more than another half an hour tonight."

Claude sighed. "All right, if I'll have you tomorrow afternoon and evening. But you better dig that wine, honey. Time's a-wasting."

He stood up and stretched, then—while he remembered—he took five crisp new ten dollar bills from his wallet and put them on the table. Rose, he thought, would take better care of it than he would. Sure, he was going to change and straighten up, but no use tempting himself too much right off the bat. Responsibility is something to get used to gradually, not all at once.

Rose was pouring the chilled wine. She put two little glasses of it on the coffee table beside the chair. She said, "I'll write that receipt and get it out of the way."

He said, "To hell with the receipt, honey. Come here." He reached but she eluded him and went over to the little writing table. He sighed and sat down again.

Scratch, scratch, went the pen. How silly of Rose to want to make out that receipt and give it to him.

Let's see, he thought, starting with that fifty, how much could he give Rose to save for him before the first of June. At ten dollars a week—hell, he could give her more than that if he took some of the overtime the boss was always trying to give him. If he took overtime, he could easily average twenty-five a week more than he'd been making—and have less time to spend it foolishly. Say he did that and saved thirty-five a week, in three and a half months, with that fifty to start, that'd be over five hundred bucks. Not bad.

And if he kept on at that rate after they were married and if Rose worked too for a while—why, it wouldn't be long before they could have a little house of their own and—*but your freedom*, something screamed inside him, *tied down, like those other poor suckers, watching dimes*—

Rose came back with the receipt. He stuffed it into his wallet without looking at it, then pulled her down into his lap again. She leaned forward, picked up a glass of wine and handed it to him, then took the other herself, touched his glass with it.

"To us, Claude."

"To us, honey," he said. He drank down the wine in two swallows so he could get rid of the glass. He didn't like wine much anyway, but Rose didn't care for either beer or whisky so he'd settled for bringing wine.

He started to pull Rose closer, realized he'd make her spill wine from the glass she held. "Drink up, honey," he said. "We haven't got much— Say, what about that telephone repair guy who was going to come around?"

"If he comes after half past eight, after you leave, he'll just have to come some other time."

"Maybe they found the trouble at the exchange. That call from your boss a few minutes ago got through all right."

"That's probably it." Rose nodded. "I said I'd be home all evening, but they wouldn't send a man *late* in the evening. They probably got it fixed."

"Rose, honey—"

She took another sip from her glass, then put it down on the coffee table and let him pull her close and kiss her. Her arms went around him and pulled him tighter. It was a long kiss, and she didn't break or try to break until Claude moved his lips away. He said, "whew!" humorously, but his eyes were shining and his arms around her were almost convulsively tight.

"Claude darling, I love you so much," Rose said. Her eyes were closed, her face very white and still.

"Gee, honey—" He was breathing a little hard and this time it wasn't humorous pretense. He kissed her closed eyelids very gently and then, with his cheek against hers, he whispered, "Oh Rose, do we have to wait?" Before she could answer his lips were on hers again and his hand moved gently to cup the soft swell of a breast.

"Rose, oh *Rose!*" he whispered. This was going to be it;

she wasn't going to make him wait any longer. The very thought of having her *now* set him on fire.

But then she was whispering, "Please, Claude, please dear—" and gently disengaging herself. But her hand tightened over his, pressing it harder a moment against her breast before she took it away.

"Claude, dear." Her voice was a little breathless, a little tremulous. "Don't kiss me for a minute, let me tell you something. You may have thought I'm cold, darling, because I haven't let you touch me. I'm *not*. When you've touched me even a *little*, it's made me want you so—so damned bad. I didn't dare let you pet me, didn't even dare let myself go when we kissed, because I wouldn't have been able to stop there—"

"But why do you—did you want to stop there? Honey, we're getting *married*."

"But I wasn't sure, dear, until tonight. I don't mean I wasn't sure I loved you—I've loved you for weeks. But—I wasn't sure of *you*. Even after last Sunday night—I thought you might want to change your mind. I knew you didn't really want to get married, have to settle down. I thought you might want to back out—"

"Back out?" He was horrified at the thought; nothing had ever been farther from his mind.

"I know, I'm sure now, Claude. Sure that you're sure. But—not tonight, dear. For two reasons, and one of them is that I'll just *have* to get to sleep early to get up at four o'clock. But if you want, tomorrow night—when we'll have all the time we want—"

If he wanted! He pulled her close again, kissed her again, and this time made his hands behave. It took will power to do it, but he did. Tomorrow night seemed a long way off—but nothing like the four months till June. And if, so wonderfully, Rose was promising him tomorrow night then the least he could do was not to try to make her yield tonight. And besides if he tried and didn't succeed, he'd just be torturing both of them.

At half past eight Rose poured them each another drink of the chilled wine and ten minutes later, after a lingering, promisefully passionate kiss at the door, he was on his way.

A bit drunk, but not from the two little glasses of wine.

He didn't feel them in the slightest degree. But he lurched once going down the stairs and grabbed the banister to regain his balance.

Outside in the quiet evening, just getting fully dark, he stood still for a moment on the sidewalk, taking in deep breaths of the coolish air. Then he crossed the street to his car and got in behind the wheel. Turned on the ignition and goosed the starter. It responded sluggishly; probably the battery was low. Well, tomorrow morning he'd check that, check over the whole damn car from bumper to bumper.

The engine caught, finally, just when he'd begun to worry that it might not. He turned on the lights and held out his hand to signal the pull-out, then suddenly wondered where he was going. Home? Before nine o'clock?

Hell no, it was too damned early to go home, on a big night like this one, a night when he felt so damned happy. He wanted a drink, to celebrate.

Oh, not to hang one on. He was changing all that now, and saving his money. No more heavy drinking, no more heavy gambling, no more betting the ponies—except maybe an occasional small bet, a buck or two, just for the fun of picking them. A reformed character, that's what he was going to be from here on in, a guy who was going to get somewhere and quit being a no-good and a rolling stone. Fifty dollars he had saved already and it was where he couldn't get at it even if he weakened. Not that he was going to weaken, not now that he really knew how much he loved Rose and how much she loved him.

Jesus, and he'd been worrying that maybe she was frigid when all the time she'd been wanting him as badly as he'd been wanting her, wanting him so badly that she hadn't dared let him do any playing around, more than having his arms around her or kissing her. Until she was sure that *he* was sure about wanting to marry her. Well, he was sure now, all right. He loved her like crazy and there wasn't a doubt left in him about his wanting to marry her, about his *needing* her in every way, including her help in straightening out the mess he'd been making out of his life until now.

But that didn't mean he couldn't have a drink—even two or three, as long as it wasn't more than that—to celebrate. Tonight was the turning point in his life. More important to him inwardly than last Sunday night when he'd popped

the question, even more important than tomorrow night—
not that it didn't make him tingle all over to think what was
going to happen *then*. But tonight was the night when he'd
found out that he was really in love and was really loved,
and when he'd really made (he'd only been thinking about
it before) the momentous decision that he was going to
change his whole way of thinking and living.

Voluntarily and happily and not because he was being
trapped into it.

Sure, he was going to have a drink on it. Where? It didn't
matter, except that he wouldn't go to either of the two
places he usually did his drinking in. He didn't, tonight,
want to see any of the gang he usually drank with and
maybe get talked into a poker game and play most of the
night. He was through with that stuff. So any tavern he
happened to pass on the way home would do.

He pulled out onto Pico and headed west, turned south
on Main before he realized that he was only a few blocks
from home and that there weren't any taverns nearby
except the two he'd decided to avoid. But he remembered
one on Ocean Front near the pier and kept on going, found
a place to park right in front of it.

Business was slow in the tavern, only five customers.
Four of them consisted of two couples in a booth, the other
a flashily dressed, paunchy man who stood at one end of
the bar talking to the white-aproned barkeeper. There was a
pad of paper and a pencil on the bar between them, Claude
noticed, and no drink. Probably, he decided, the paunchy
man was a liquor salesman. Not that it mattered. He went
to the other end of the bar and sat on a stool. The bartender
came over.

"Bourbon and soda," Claude told him. "Easy on the
soda. Hell, make it a double while you're at it." He was
only going to have one or two anyway.

The bartender nodded and reached for the bar whiskey
bottle. Two glasses clinked together back in the booth and a
man's voice called out, "Hey, another round same way."
"Coming up," the bartender called back. He put Claude's
drink in front of him and motioned with his eyes toward the
booth. "Know what that gang's ordering? One Manhattan,
one old-fashioned, one martini, one daiquiri. Four people,
four different cocktails. Anything to make a man work."

Claude grinned at him. "It's a tough life, my friend."

The bartender grunted and started in to fill the order. Behind him, in the backbar mirror, Claude saw the door open and close as a man, alone, came in and came toward the bar. He slid onto the stool two stools away from Claude's. "A beer when you get time," the newcomer told the bartender. "Eastern. Schlitz, if you got it."

"I got it and I got time," the bartender said. He put bottle and glass on the bar and then went back to his job on the four different cocktails.

Without particular interest—except that something looked vaguely familiar about him—Claude looked at the man who had just come in and who was now pouring beer from the bottle into the glass. About Claude's own height, he'd noticed in the mirror as the man had come in, fairly husky-looking shoulders, a roundish face. Felt hat pulled down all around. Gray suit.

No, he didn't know the guy. Just something about him reminded him of someone he knew or had met recently.

He looked down at his own drink and took a sip of it. It tasted good and took the wine taste out of his mouth.

But thinking of the wine made him think of Rose again—not that he'd ever really stopped thinking about her for more than a few seconds at a time—and he sighed a little, almost audibly.

Tomorrow. Tomorrow night. Voluptuous pictures ran through his mind and for a moment he tried to stop them, then wondered why he had tried or why he should try. This wasn't any sordid affair, this was love, real love, the works. And sex and desire were part of it but there was nothing dirty about that. The fact that they were getting married made all the difference.

Tomorrow night, really, they were getting married. The papers they'd sign and the words they'd say early in June were just papers and words. Tomorrow night was what counted.

Where would it happen? In Rose's little apartment, or would they go to a motel after driving around a while? He thought about the advantages and disadvantages of each. If he took her to a motel would she be more or less likely to be willing to spend the night, all of the night, with him than she would be to let him stay all night at her place? It should be all night, it very much should be all night the first time. Like a honeymoon, the whole night together. And he thought Rose felt the same way about it; that's why she hadn't let it happen tonight when he couldn't have stayed long anyway.

In one way at least her room would be better. It would set a precedent. A motel would be fine but a lot of motels between now and June would run to a lot of money. And he was supposed to be saving money. Yes, going back to her room would be better, setting the precedent of his staying there. Thank God it wasn't just a rooming house like his with a landlady who knew everything that went on. Her room—room and a half, really—was at least private. Nobody checked people in and out and Rose didn't even know her neighbors so nobody would know the difference, no matter how often or late he stayed, as long as they were reasonably discreet.

God, he thought, if it were only tomorrow evening at this time.

And maybe he could talk Rose out of going to work Sunday—she was going to quit that damned waitress job anyway and get into an office again so what the hell—and they could spend the whole week end, stay together right through Sunday—

Oh, Lord, he'd made a date with Joyce Williams for Sunday afternoon and she was going to phone him at noon on Sunday.

Why had he done something so crazy as that, when he was engaged to Rose and head over heels in love with Rose? Just impulse. He hadn't been thinking. Running into Joyce like that after not having seen her for so many years, it had just seemed the natural thing to do. And with Rose working an afternoon and into-the-evening shift that day, it had seemed a perfect opportunity to take Joyce for a spin.

What was he going to do about it now, though?

Not just stand Joyce up; that was for sure. She was too nice a kid for that. No matter how the week end worked out between Rose and himself, he'd have to be home at the rooming house at noon to take Joyce's call. And let her off gently by telling her—well, any story that wouldn't hurt her pride.

Or if Rose insisted on going to work, if he couldn't talk

her out of it, there wasn't any reason why he shouldn't take Joyce for a spin in the car at that. It could be perfectly innocent and he could break it to her that he was engaged now, that he'd wanted to see her again for old times' sake but that this would have to be the only time. There'd be nothing disloyal to Rose in his doing that.

He looked down at his drink and saw that it was empty. Should he order another double, he wondered. Hell, he thought, why not? Why shouldn't he get gloriously drunk, if he wanted to, to celebrate? This was his last *bachelor* night. Tomorrow night he'd be as good as married, and that would be the time to turn over his new leaf, cut down on drinking and extravagance.

But did he really want to get drunk? Well, he'd wait and see on that, but meanwhile—

The bartender was back talking to the flashily dressed man. But he happened to glance toward Claude and Claude nodded. "Another," he said, "a double," when the bartender came over to him.

He took a sip and then sat staring into his glass, wondering if he really should get drunk tonight, make it a final binge, a real last bachelor night. But if so, this would be his last drink here; he didn't know anybody here and he didn't like solitary drinking—beyond a drink or two, anyway. He'd go back home first and put his car in the garage so he wouldn't have to drive it home afterwards and then go to one of the places within walking distance, places where he knew other guys and would find someone to drink with.

Yes, this would be his last drink here. And he suddenly remembered that he hadn't paid for it yet, or for the first one. He took out his wallet and extracted a bill, a crisp new ten, one of the ones Joyce had given him when she'd cashed Conn's check for him. He put it on the bar.

Then picked up his drink to finish it fairly quickly and get going. Home, in any case, and then decide whether or not he wanted to go out again afoot and really hang one on.

"Pardon me."

Claude turned his head and saw that it was the man who had come in a few minutes ago who was talking to him, from two stools away. He had a wallet in his hand and was taking a bill from it. "That's a ten you just put on the bar, isn't it?" the man with the roundish face asked.

"Sure," Claude said.

"Wonder if you mind if I take it for an old worn-out bill." The stranger smiled. "I wanted to get to the bank before it closed to get a new ten dollar bill and didn't make it in time. It's for a present—my nephew's birthday tomorrow. And when you give money it ought to be a crisp new bill, not an old one.

"Sure, help yourself," Claude said.

The stranger reached over and changed the bills. He took an envelope from his pocket and put the new bill into it. "It'll keep it clean," he said. "Drink up and have one with me."

"Thanks, but I was just getting ready to go when I finished this one. Thanks just the same."

"Hell, you can drink one more. Me, I'm celebrating tonight."

Claude started to say he was celebrating too and then changed his mind. If he said that, he'd be stuck with this guy and he didn't know whether he liked him yet. There was something funny about the guy, although he couldn't put his finger on just what it was.

So he settled for, "Yeah?" and since that didn't sound like quite enough when he'd just been offered a drink, he added "Celebrating what?"

"Bought myself back into business today. A garage, over on Wilshire."

"The hell," said Claude, interested. "Good luck. You mean a repair garage?"

"Yes. Good location near Douglas Park. Fairly new building, plenty of room to expand. It's been keeping three mechanics busy but the guy who owned it is a schmoe; I'll be doing twice his business in a few months. Place will be a gold mine if I can find the right man for a service manager. Sure you won't change your mind on that drink?"

"Thanks," Claude said. "I guess I will." He caught the bartender's eye and motioned to him. The bartender came over.

The roundish faced man put a five on the bar. "His drink's on me," he told the bartender. "And I'll have another beer."

He turned back to Claude. "Hell of a thing to have to celebrate on beer but it's doctor's orders, no hard liquor for another two months. Getting over ulcers. You know Grand Rapids, Michigan?"

Claude shook his head.

"I had a service garage there, doing all right with it. But I got a good offer for it two months ago and I sold. On account of I've always wanted to live in California, see? And that was my chance to sell out there and buy here. Been looking around out here ever since and found this place for sale just a few days ago. Closed the deal on it today."

"Hasn't it got a service manager?" Claude asked. "Or is he quitting?"

"Guy I'm buying from has been handling that part of it himself. I can handle the office end okay, but I'm a businessman and not a mechanic and a good service manager's got to be, or have been, a mechanic." He poured more beer into his glass from the bottle. "Maybe I'll send a wire tomorrow to the boy I had managing for me back in Michigan. He might want to come out here—if I made him a good proposition."

"What would the job pay?" Claude asked.

His companion turned and looked at him. "Mean you're interested? Is that your line of work?"

"I'm damned interested. No, I've never been a service manager, but I'm a good mechanic. Seven years' experience, pretty much all-around except body and fender work. And I know pretty much about estimating already from working in small shops where I helped the boss with that end of it."

My God, what a break, he was thinking, if this should work out; if he could get this job tonight would *really* be the turning point in his life. Surely the job wouldn't start at less than a hundred and if the shop was going to be expanding, he'd be making a hell of a lot more than that pretty soon. And how swell it would be to be able to hand Rose the news tomorrow night, prove to her already that her faith in him was justified and that he was starting to go places. He watched his companion's face eagerly.

"Well—I'd had in mind a man with *some* experience as a service manager, but—I don't know, maybe you could pick it up pretty quick. You working now?"

"Sure, at Purdy's—on Lincoln in Venice. But it's a big

place and they wouldn't miss me if I had to give them short notice, or no notice at all, for that matter."

"Worked there long?"

"Only a couple of months." Claude hesitated and then took the plunge, told the truth about himself, that thus far he'd never worked very long—six months was about the longest—at any one place, and that he'd done quite a bit of drifting from job to job and taking time off when he had one.

"You can call any of the places I worked," he said, "here or in San Diego or San Francisco and they'll all tell you I'm a damn good mechanic—and they may tell you I'm not very steady. But here's the thing—I just got engaged, going to be married the first week in June. So I've got to settle down and *be* steady. A break like getting even a chance to try out as a service manager is just what I need. I'd work my head off to make a go of it, and of the shop."

"Hmmm. You might be just the guy I'm looking for at that. Anyway, we can talk about it some more. One thing you got, anyway, the right kind of looks and personality for the job. The service manager's the one who talks to the customer so he's got to have a good front. There are two out of the three mechs working there now who might be worth trying out for the job except for that. Both good grease monkeys but one of them barely talks English so you can understand him and the other—well, he's sullen and short-tempered; he'd get into too many arguments with the customers."

"I've done a little selling," Claude said. "Maybe I'm not as hot a salesman as I am a mechanic, but at least I can talk to people." He grinned. "Enough to convince at least some of them their cars need twice as much work as they'd thought."

"Sounds like you know the racket already. Say, how about another drink?"

"Let me buy a round," Claude said. "Say, my name's Atkins, Claude Atkins."

His name was William Pierce, Conn told Atkins. And added that Atkins' money was no good; *he* was the one who was celebrating and all drinks were on him.

He'd sure picked the right story, Conn was thinking, to get Atkins interested. Now, for as long as he could string Atkins along without actually promising him the job or completely discouraging him on his chances of getting it, Atkins would stick to him like a brother for the rest of the evening.

It was a break, of course, pure luck that Atkins had just got engaged and was turning over a new leaf; it made him *really* want that job. But it should have been adequate bait even under more ordinary circumstances. Anybody is interested in a job that pays a lot more than he's making, if he thinks he can handle that job. And probably nine mechanics out of ten think they could make good service managers if they had the chance.

Besides, Conn figured, he was due for a little good luck after the horribly bad luck of having seen Atkins leave the girl's place so damned early. Ten or fifteen minutes later and Conn would have been ready and waiting under the stairs; it would all be over now. Why in God's name had Atkins left his girl so incredibly early, especially if they'd just become engaged. A quarrel? Hardly, Atkins seemed too cheerful and happy just to have had a fight with his fiancée and besides any quarrel serious enough to have made him walk out on her would probably have ended the engagement, especially a recent engagement. Well, that didn't matter now. For whatever reason, it had happened. And Conn had had no trouble at all following the yellow convertible.

But it would have been so simple in the hallway, as he had planned it.

And what horribly bad luck that he hadn't gone back to the shop and got the sixty-odd dollars from the cashbox before he'd started out. He'd decided, and quite logically, that it would be impossible to approach Atkins and try to buy those nine bills back from him with genuine ones.

But he'd bought back one of them already, and without arousing the slightest suspicion. Surely, especially now that he had Atkins' full interest and confidence, had Atkins hanging on every word and eager to please, he could think up some story to account for his wanting more crisp, new bills—for presents or whatever—and ask Atkins to look and see if he had any more as fresh as the first one.

But he had only thirty-two dollars left now instead of ninety-odd to buy back the rest of the bills. Did he dare risk leaving Atkins here—saying he had an appointment and would be back in half an hour to resume the celebration?

No, it would give Atkins too much time to think, to wonder why a man who had just announced he was starting to celebrate would suddenly remember an appointment. Or Atkins might volunteer to drive him to the appointment and he couldn't take Atkins to the printing shop. Or—no, there were too many wheels that might come off if he left Atkins alone now that he'd made the contact. At the very least Atkins would have time to build up a suspicion, however slight, of the fortuitousness of the encounter. And if, after that, he tried to trade Atkins out of eight more ten dollar bills, Atkins would suspect he was being tricked somehow—probably he'd suspect the very opposite of the truth, that this new-found friend was trying to buy genuine bills from him for counterfeit ones.

Yes, the only thing he could do now was stick with Atkins until he could get him alone and either knock him out or hold him up. And the former would be the safer, if he could do it. Atkins somehow didn't look to be the type of man who'd be too afraid of a gun or a holdup, who might all too easily make a grab for the gun instead of putting up his hands quietly. Especially when he had on him what would seem to him to be a considerable chunk of cash.

What would be the safest thing? Suggest another tavern—a livelier one—accept Atkins' offer of a lift there (the sedan was parked half a block away and he could pretend that he had come here afoot or by taxi) and then, in the car—?

It might work, but not at this end of the trip. The convertible was parked in a brightly lighted spot and with the top down. And this early in the evening there were too many people on the street. . . .

". . . been trying to think who you remind me of," Atkins was saying. "Someone I've seen recently."

"Might have seen me," Conn suggested. "I've been looking over a lot of garages out this way in the last month or so—even ones that weren't for sale, just to get the general picture. I don't specially remember the one you mentioned by name, but I've looked through a couple of hundred of them."

Atkins shook his head. "I don't think so, Mr. Pierce. It isn't that I feel I've seen *you*. It's just that something about you, I don't know just what, reminds me of someone— Hell, I got it."

"Who?"

"Guy I traded cars with last night. A printer, got a shop over on Santa Monica Boulevard. Darius somebody, I forget his last name." He was frowning. "Funny, damn if I know *why* you remind me of him; you're bigger and—well, the top part of your face is like his, but even outside of that— Oh well, it doesn't matter, now that I've thought of it. Just one of those things you have to think of before you can forget them."

No, Conn thought, it didn't matter at all—except now he'd have to kill Atkins, not just rob him. He sighed. Well, it was probably safer to kill anyway. There would always have been the chance that Atkins, thinking back afterwards, would have arrived at the connection somehow.

Murder is a cleaner, safer crime.

And more merciful than most crimes, Conn thought, if it is done mercifully and without making the victim suffer. He'd worked out a philosophy about it, of course, before he'd found himself suddenly a murderer.

Since then, he'd been interested. He'd started buying fact crime magazines for his light reading, and he'd read every one of the books in the Santa Monica Public Library that concerned crime in general or murder in particular. *Real* murder, that is; detective and mystery novels didn't interest him at all now, although before his experience of a year ago he'd read them avidly in what little leisure time he'd had for reading. Now they seemed to him to be artificial and contrived, divorced completely from reality.

He'd started taking a daily newspaper too (before that he'd settled for getting his news from a weekly newsmagazine and occasional radio newscasts) and found himself quite interested in following current crime cases, solved and unsolved. (Books on crime, he'd noticed, concentrated mostly on solved crimes; from the newspapers one realized how many crimes are never solved.)

Crime interested him and criminals interested him and he read about both. But the thing that interested him most was what was *not* written about—the man behind the *unsolved* crime, the criminal who was never discovered. The Perfect Criminal. The Man Who Got Away With It.

Gradually a picture of him built up. Not of his physical appearance; that was irrelevant. He might be four feet tall or seven, fat or thin, old or young. You couldn't even guess what he might seem like to those who knew him (but, of course, did not guess that he was a criminal). He might seem dashing or stodgy, brilliant or dull, loquacious or quiet. There would be no way of identifying him from without.

But the Perfect Criminal would have patience and the ability to plan ahead, as Conn planned his counterfeiting. But planning wasn't enough; he must have the ability to think fast and think straight, as Conn had thought when he had found that he had killed his wife. He must have courage and calm, as Conn had proved himself to have on that same occasion. He must be able to think quickly and be able to change his plans quickly, as Conn had been able to change his plans to take Atkins in the hallway on Pico into what he was doing now. He must be able to improvise rapidly and plausibly, as Conn had done in getting the first of those nine bills off the bar and into his pocket a few minutes ago. He must have calm confidence in himself, as Conn had now. The thinking processes of the Perfect Criminal, in fact, had a very strong resemblance to the thinking processes of Darius Conn, successful murderer and soon to be successful and well-to-do counterfeiter.

Never panic; that was the main rule. Stay cool, stay calm, and think.

He was thinking hard now, wondering what his next move should be. Running over in his mind, among other things, various other taverns he knew of and could suggest going to, thinking of them particularly in terms of how well lighted the parking areas around them would be. No, this early in the evening all of them would be too dangerous. Damn the fact that they'd be in an *open* car. And it would simply have to be the convertible; even if he got blind drunk Atkins would probably recognize the sedan that had been his until only yesterday evening.

Think. Improvise.

He needed a quiet side street in a residential district, not too well lighted. But the suggestion that would take them there didn't have to be the suggestion to go to a tavern, although that could be the bait at the end of the line. A private house—his brother's house, since he'd already said he had a nephew—to pick up something, some papers, that he was going to need and had left there. Suggest a tavern a couple of miles away. On the way there, suddenly remark that if Atkins didn't mind would he let him stop in just a second at his brother's house to get something he'd left there. . . . "Just a couple of blocks from here. Forget the exact address but I've been there often enough. It's just up this side street." Pick the darkest quietest spot on a quiet street and tell Atkins, "That's the house. Park right there; I won't be half a minute." And, with his right hand, get the gun out of his pocket ready to swing and at the instant when Atkins parked and leaned forward to turn the ignition key . . .

"Huh?" he said. Atkins was turning around to get off the stool and he'd just said something Conn had missed.

Atkins grinned. "Just said I was going to the can a second. Excuse me." He went toward the back of the tavern, around the bar.

Quickly Conn slid off his own stool, remembering what had happened a year ago when he himself had gone out the back door of the tavern on Second Street, the night he'd sneaked away from the bank teller to go home to his wife. He didn't see any possible reason why Atkins, under these circumstances, would be heading for a back-door sneak, but if Atkins did he'd have to improvise, fast.

Glass of beer in his hand, Conn strolled over to the juke box against the side wall, pretending to look down at the orderly rows of little white cards that gave the names of the selections. Actually, out of the corner of his eye, watching Atkins' retreating back. There was a back door all right, but Atkins didn't go that far; he went through the door marked *Men* at one side of the corridor. But just on the off-chance that he was going there first and then out, Conn decided to stay at the juke box.

He fished a loose dime out of his pocket and pretended, after he had dropped it in the slot, to be choosing the two records it would give him. He reached forward to punch two buttons at random and then pulled his hand back. Might as well pick ones he really wouldn't mind hearing. At least he'd avoid cowboy or hillbilly stuff; he hated both of them. (Myrtle had loved both of them. God, how many coins he'd fed into juke boxes for her to listen to the horrible things.)

There were plenty of cowboy and hillbilly records. A few Spanish ones too; he didn't actually dislike Spanish records but they all sounded alike to him. A few old-timers, either revivals or new versions: *Stardust, Dinah, Girl of My Dreams, You Rascal You.* . . .

He heard the men's room door open and out of the corner of his eye watched Atkins come out and turn immediately to come back his way. He punched two buttons quickly and strolled back to the bar before Atkins got there.

He needn't have worried, he saw now. Atkins had left his money on the bar, the change from the ten Conn had traded him for the new one. The eight dollars and a little change after the bartender had taken out for the two doubles Atkins had ordered for himself before Conn had started buying for him.

He saw too that Atkins' glass was empty and he signaled the bartender to fill it. Atkins was sliding onto the stool beside him. "Hey," he said, "let me get a round here."

"Nuts," Conn said. "Told you it was my celebration." He saw that his own bottle of beer was more than half full and shook his head so the bartender wouldn't line him up another one.

Girl of my dreams, I love you . . .

That would be Atkins' fifth double, Conn was thinking. If Atkins got too much to drink, too fast, he wouldn't want to go to another tavern. Maybe he'd better suggest moving on as soon as Atkins had finished that one. He could start the groundwork now.

"This place is kind of dull," he said.

"Yeah," Atkins said. Absently, listening to the juke box.

*. . . your charms
Again in my arms, . . .*

Thinking about that girl of his, Conn realized. Lost and dreaming. In love.

Like he, Conn had once been in love, with Myrtle. God, why had he ever loved her at all, let alone been so damned crazy about her? She'd been a bitch.

And yet even after he'd known she was a bitch, how he'd *wanted* her.

And still did, damn it all. No other woman's body would ever be to him what Myrtle's had been, a flame. No matter how much money he ever made and no matter how many and how beautiful the women that money might bring him, never again would he know that horrible-wonderful desire he'd felt for his wife. Any other woman would be a substitute, a pale imitation.

Why, *why?*

> *Life don't seem the same,*
> *Please come back again . . .*

But she wouldn't be coming back again, ever. And if she did, she'd come back hating him; she'd hated him before he'd killed her.

God damn silly popular song. He wanted suddenly to go over and stop the juke box, smash his fist through the glass and stop the record, break it into a thousand pieces.

He made himself calm down. He had business to attend to, a murder to commit.

The Perfect Murderer is always calm.

He was calm, quite calm, watching Atkins out of the corner of his eye. The guy was still dreaming, no use talking to him until this record was over. Puppy love.

Damn the kid, why hadn't he stayed ten or fifteen minutes longer with that girl if he was so much in love with her? Then this would all be over with by now.

The record finished and Conn took a swallow of his beer. "This place is kind of dull," he said again, knowing Atkins hadn't really heard him the first time. "I know a good place over on Wilshire—"

He broke off as the second record started. Something about it— Blue music, no voice yet, but there was *something* about the music itself— He tried to remember what record he had punched for the second one.

Then the voice started, a Negro voice, deep blue.

I'll be glad when you're dead, you rascal you,

Jesus H. Christ, Conn thought, why had he punched the button for *that* song? Consciously, he'd completely forgotten what the words were, but had his subconscious mind done it?

It was howlingly funny and he wanted to laugh, but he couldn't because he wouldn't be able to explain why he was laughing. He had a momentary ridiculous picture of himself laughing and Atkins asking him why, and his explaining. "It's funny because I really *will* be glad when you're dead. You see, I've got to kill you tonight."

It was hard not to laugh.

Think about something else, think about *anything*—

Atkins saved him. Atkins was saying, "I don't know, Mr. Pierce. I mean, whether I should go anywhere to do any more drinking. I got to get up early tomorrow morning to work on my car. Got to get it fixed up for something—something pretty important I got to use it for tomorrow. And besides—well, like I said, now I'm engaged I'm turning over a new leaf. Maybe I better—"

There ain't no use to run, you rascal you,
There ain't no use to run, you rascal you.
There ain't no use to run . . .

"Oh hell," Conn said. "It's early. Not even ten o'clock yet. Evening's a pup. Listen, you really serious about wanting that job?'"

"Serious? Hell, yes, just give me a *chance* at it, Mr. Pierce. I'll work my damn fool head off to make good."

"Well—damn, I hate to say yes right off on something that important. Let's get to know one another a little better first."

"Sure. Or you want me to stop in at the garage Monday morning and talk it over? and I can start in right then if it's okay. What's the address on Wilshire?"

I'll be glad when you're dead with six feet over your head.

"You don't have to come in unless you're going to *start* in. I'll make up my mind in a minute. Damn it, don't *push*

me—uh, what'd you say your first name is?"

"Claude. Claude Atkins, Mr. Pierce."

"Okay, Claude. Call me Bill. But hell's bells, it's not ten o'clock yet. Quit worrying about tomorrow. Maybe tomorrow will never come."

Atkins laughed. "I'm not worrying about that—Bill. But I am worrying about one thing. Here I've been drinking doubles, four or five of 'em already. And sure—I've got something to celebrate too, if you give me a chance at that job. But many more of these and I'll get drunk and then you'll change your mind. You'll decide I'd make a hell of a lousy service manager for you."

Conn grinned. "You got a point there, Claude, old boy. But not too much of a point. Me I'm not a lush but I've got drunk often enough not to judge a guy by how he acts." He straightened his face out and frowned. "Of course, drinking on the *job*, that's something else. You don't do that, do you?"

"Christ, no."

"Good. About that job. Okay, you want it definite, I'll make it definite—on one condition. But first—is a hundred a week okay to start? I'll go up if you make good and if the shop makes good."

"Fine."

"Monday morning then. Shop's been opening at eight, and I'll stick to that for a while. Maybe change later. And like I said, the guy I bought from handled that end himself. He'll be in Monday and he can show you the ropes."

"Swell. What's the name of the shop and just where is it?" Conn grinned again. "That's where the condition comes in. You got to stick around with me a while—I won't keep you up late if you want to get up early—before I tell you where the goddam garage is."

Atkins put back his head and laughed. "You got me there. Okay, I'll stick around. Only I'm switching to singles instead of doubles."

"Just so you stick around a while," Conn said. "Let's have one more here and then go to the Wilshire place for one or two. Then I'll he ready to call it off."

He signaled to the bartender.

No hurry now that he could be sure Atkins would stay with him and leave when he did. Just the reverse, in fact;

the longer he waited before leaving here the fewer people there would he on the streets, the better his chances would be.

"You driving tonight?" he asked Claude.

"Yeah."

"Good. I'm not. Started out in the car and found the damn brakes weren't holding right. Went halfway across the street when I tried to stop for a stop sign. I put it right back in the garage. Get it looked at in the morning."

"Probably sprung a leak in the lines," Atkins said. "Losing your fluid. If you got hydraulics, I mean."

"That's it. Brake pedal went way down. Think I know when it happened, earlier in the afternoon. Hit a stone and the tire flipped it up under the car, hell of a clunk it made. Probably cracked a line or loosened a connection."

"Yeah. Well, my car's a jalopy but it'll get us around." Atkins grinned. "Don't judge me as a mechanic by the way it runs, though. Just made a swap for it last night and it needs a tune-up and some other work and I haven't had time to touch it yet. Worked till four-thirty and then had to rush home and clean up for a dinner date."

"Sure you're sober enough to drive?" Conn asked. The sudden thought had come to him that it just might he safer to persuade Atkins to garage his car, with the story that they'd use a taxi thereafter. He could go along, of course, and if Atkins kept it in a nice private garage then what he had to do would be a hell of a lot safer than on the street.

"I'm okay," Atkins said, "unless I drink a hell of a lot more than this."

"Good. Where do you live, by the way?"

"Ten blocks or so north of here. Just off Main Street. A rooming house."

"Good place? I've been staying with my brother till now—for all I knew until today I'd be buying a business in Long Beach or out in the valley or somewhere so no use looking for a place to live till I knew where I'd be working. But I can't stay with him forever."

"It's a fair place. Fair for the money, I mean. But no vacancies right now."

"A rooming house might be a good bet for me, though. I hate hotels. How do places around here handle garage

space, though? Is that furnished or do you got to rent a garage on your own?"

"Not furnished where I room. But I don't have to rent one. Empty lot right across the street, several of us park there. Right by a street lamp, good and light; car's as safe there as it would be anywhere."

"Oh," Conn said. Well, that possibility was out. And he'd be in a jam now if Atkins should decide he wasn't sober enough to drive.

Atkins' drink—he'd ordered a single this time—was about half gone. Conn picked up his beer and started working on it so he'd finish about the same time Atkins did. No use stalling any longer than that. Might as well get it over with.

He was quite calm, completely confident and unafraid.

When Atkins picked up his glass again Conn said, "Whenever you're ready."

"Sure. Ready now." Atkins finished the rest of his drink. He picked up his money from the bar, put the change in his pocket and the bills into his wallet. Conn tried to get a look inside the wallet while it was open, but the angle was wrong; he caught the flash of a new bill on top but couldn't see how many there were. But what was he worrying about, he asked himself. The money was all there. From the printing shop, Atkins had gone right to his room to dress and then to his girl's place for dinner. And he'd broken a ten to pay for the two drinks he'd ordered for himself, which meant he hadn't broken one before. And even if he had, *one* bad ten might lead suspicion where Conn didn't want it to be led, but it wouldn't be proof of anything.

"Parked right in front," Atkins said. "That old yellow job."

They got off their stools, walked toward the front. "Thanks, fellas," the bartender said. "Come back again."

"We will," Conn told him.

Conn opened the door on the curb side, the familiar handle that he'd turned thousands of times. Have to remember fingerprints afterwards, he thought. Not that a few fingerprints here or there should matter too much since he'd owned the car himself until last night, but there shouldn't be too many fresh ones on top. Atkins was getting in on the driver's side. Slammed the door with the familiar tinny sound the door on that side had always had.

Atkins stepped on the starter and the engine turned over sluggishly. "Give it a little more choke." He added, "I had a model just like this once—except it was a coupe. They need plenty of choke."

Atkins pulled out the choke and the engine caught. "Say, you're right."

He turned north on Main, east on Pico. He still drove easily and well, Conn was glad to see. It seemed strange to be riding here on the passenger side of the old boat. Where Myrtle always sat. He'd bought this car—used then, but a lot newer than it was now—while he'd been going with Myrtle, before they were married. Because she'd wanted a convertible, had been crazy about a convertible. Before then, for several years he'd been getting by without a car. He'd been rooming so near the printing shop that he hadn't really needed one. Not having a car let him keep more capital in the business and God knows the business had needed every cent of capital he could leave in it. As it was, he'd had to buy paper stock in such small quantities that it had cost him fancy prices. And if you pay fancy prices for paper how can you compete with shops that get it cheaper by buying in quantity?

But he'd come to like the car, except for its being a convertible. Myrtle had never liked it, although she hadn't told him so before they were married.

Nearing Lincoln Atkins slowed down. "Whereabouts on Wilshire is this tavern? Should I cut over here?"

"Yes, turn here," Conn said.

And in a moment now when they'd made the turn, would be the time for him to say—he started to work out the wording in his mind—*Say, it won't be out of the way to go past my brother's house and there's something I want to pick up there. Would you mind dropping me off just a second?*

And then he'd tell Atkins to turn off on Michigan and then turn again on one of the numbered streets, the side streets . . . An alley would be even better. But could he, logically, suggest turning into an alley? A rear cottage, maybe? Then the better idea came to him.

"Say, Claude," he said. "How'd you like a quick look at where you're going to work? It's not out of our way."

"Swell. That would be swell. Where on Wilshire?"

"Across from Douglas Park, but damn if I remember the street number. But I'll tell you how to get there. Turn up Arizona and we'll cut through the alley and park behind it. I've got the key to the back door and we'll go in that way. I want to look the place over again myself."

He watched the side streets on Arizona Avenue. Where was Douglas Park? Oh yes, at Chelsea Street. Just past Twenty-fourth, he said, "Turn in the alley here, Claude. That's it."

A block ahead of them. Wilshire. An occasional car going by. Have to stop before they reached it or Atkins would see that there wasn't a garage on either corner of the alley.

He watched closely. Fifty yards, about, before they reached Wilshire he saw open space to his right, a loading zone. "In here and park," he said. And as Atkins turned off the alley, "The garage lot's off Wilshire, other side of the building, but since I got the back door key, this'll do."

He had the revolver out of his pocket now, gripping it butt outward in his right hand, a good firm grip. He half turned in the seat. Watched while Atkins pulled out the hand brake, shut off the ignition and the lights and then turned to open the door on his side of the car.

Conn swung the gun. It hit hard with a *thunking* sound. Atkins fell forward, his forehead striking the edge of the car door with a second but fainter *thunk;* he slumped down sidewise in the seat.

Utter silence then. Conn could hear the sound of his own breathing, just a bit faster than usual.

Be calm now, think. First things first. Make sure Atkins is dead. He shifted the gun to his left hand and with his right reached around and under Atkins. Got his hand inside the coat and fumbled with a shirt button until he got it unbuttoned, reached inside. No undershirt. No heartbeat that he could find, and he took his time making sure, making very sure. There was no hurry now.

Next, the wallet. Right hip pocket, he'd carried it. He had to move Atkins a little to get at it, but not very far. Too dark here to look into it or count the bills, but he wasn't worried about that. If Atkins had broken one of the other tens, between the printing shop and his girl's place, it was too late to do anything about it now and anyway the chance of it being traced back to him was slight. He put the wallet into his own pocket. It was his inside coat pocket with the envelope that had contained eleven of the twenty bills and that now contained twelve of them, with the one he'd bought back over the bar.

Fingerprints? Yes, he'd use his handkerchief to wipe off the door handle and the top edge of the door on his side; they were the only smooth surfaces he'd touched. But he'd do that from outside the car so he wouldn't have to touch them again afterwards.

But he should make it look more like a robbery by going through Atkins' other pockets, taking his wrist watch, leaving the glove compartment door open to show he'd gone through it too. With a bit of difficulty he pulled Atkins back upright in the seat and went through his other pockets, found nothing else a real robber might have taken except the wrist watch. He put that in his side coat pocket. And again made sure—very sure—that there was no heartbeat.

Was there anything else he should do? Yes, get the body down on the floor, as far out of sight as possible. The longer before it was found the better, not that there was much chance of it being found before morning anyway. He took care of that, partly from outside the car so the floor would be clear. Then he closed the door of the car and took care of fingerprints on it with his handkerchief.

Stood there a moment in the darkness, waiting for his breathing to become completely normal after the exertion of moving the body. And thinking, too, taking his time to think, to make sure, absolutely sure that he was leaving nothing undone, leaving no clue behind that might lead the police to him.

Oh, the police would come to him, no doubt, possibly as soon as sometime tomorrow. They'd be checking all of Atkins' friends, acquaintances, people he'd done business with. And the change of registration on the car would show it to have been Conn's and that the transfer had happened only the day before Atkins' death, so they'd reach him, through routine and ask him routine questions. But, by then, there'd be nothing—not even if they brought a search warrant and searched his house and the printing shop both—nothing whatsoever to tie him to Atkins. Or to cause them to suspect him of counterfeiting.

Sure he'd traded cars with Atkins. Had given him ninety dollars difference. (He'd better tell them that lest Atkins had told some of his friends or his girl about the deal.) But there would be no reason for them to doubt his story that was the only time in his life that he'd ever seen Atkins. No reason for them to suspect him of a motive for murder.

And before they reached him for that routine check, there'd be no counterfeit money either at his house or at the printing shop, no indication that there had ever been any made, no disguises, no gun. no indication of anything to make them suspicious.

Alibi? He didn't need an alibi this time. Home in bed, asleep. If they even asked him where he'd been.

Breathing quietly now, perfectly calm, he walked through the rest of the alley onto Wilshire. Turned west.

An empty taxicab went by and for a second he considered hailing it, but then didn't. If he took a cab to get back to his car, still parked half a block from the tavern near Ocean Park Pier, he shouldn't take one from so near the spot where the body would be found in the morning. The police might check cab drivers for pickups in this neighborhood around the time of the crime. And while he was still in disguise and the description a cab driver would give wouldn't fit Darius Conn, there was no use leaving more of a trail than he had to.

He'd walk at least half a dozen blocks before he took a cab. He could even walk all the way back to his car if he wanted to; it would take him half an hour, maybe three-quarters, but there was no hurry. He'd still be home before midnight.

It might be best to walk, at that. He thought well while walking, especially at night. And while he was sure he'd done nothing wrong thus far, it would be well to think ahead and figure all his coming moves carefully.

The neighbors, for instance; what if someone saw him coming home tonight and what if he told the police he'd been been home all evening? No, he could dismiss that as negligible. First, because the police wouldn't have enough cause for suspicion to check with his neighbors; second, because his neighbors were go-to-bed-early people, all of them, probably sound asleep already. And none of them were snoopy anyway or paid any attention to his comings and goings. Mrs. Korbinski, the woman who'd seen Myrtle's lover enter and leave that night a year ago, had been a snoop (and thank God that she had been, that night!) but she'd moved away four months ago.

Yes, barring sheer accident, he was in the clear. Or would be before the police reached him.

And even sheer accident— It had been sheer unforeseeable accident that had put those nine counterfeit bills into Atkins' hands in the first place, hadn't it? He'd got around that, hadn't he? And when, because of Atkins having left his girl's place so ridiculously early, his first plan had missed out, he'd managed to improvise and come up with just as good a plan, hadn't he? An even better one, really, because in the dark parking place off the alley he'd been able to take his time and be careful; in a lighted hallway he'd have been hurried, and there would have been the possibility, however slight, of someone else entering or leaving the building at the same time Atkins left.

He felt pretty good, pretty well satisfied with himself and with the way he'd handled things tonight.

He was sorry that he'd had to kill but he had really had to. And he'd done it cleanly, neatly, and mercifully.

In all the reading about crime he'd done in the last year, he'd found that only one type of crime had repelled him— the murder in which the victim was made to suffer needlessly before his death. Conn had always hated pain for others as well as for himself. Thinking back after he had killed her, he had been glad Myrtle's death had been completely painless for her. She would not have had time to feel pain from the clean blow that had knocked her unconscious, and she had never regained consciousness at all. She hadn't felt his hands choking out her life, and since she hadn't even known that she was dying, she had not felt fear either.

In a way it had been as perfect and as peaceful a death as that of someone who dies quietly in his sleep. Unknowing, unsuspecting, without a moment of fear or pain or regret. A perfect death.

And Atkins' death had been even cleaner. One instant he'd been alive and happy. The next instant dead. And without transition of even a second's duration. How many people die as easily as Atkins had just died?

Another empty cab, but he was almost to Lincoln Avenue now and decided he might as well get off Wilshire before he took one, if he was going to take one at all. He was enjoying the walk.

And enjoying—well, not enjoying what he had just done; he'd rather liked Claude Atkins—but enjoying and feeling proud of the craftsmanlike and merciful way in which he'd done it.

And thinking regretfully how lonesome a thing it is to be a murderer, to have perfectly accomplished a skillful and difficult act, and to be able to discuss it with no one, brag about it nowhere. Was that why so many criminals ran in *gangs*, so they'd have friends they could trust to admire their exploits? He knew that wasn't the reason and yet felt amusement at the thought.

He should be damned unhappy about tonight, he realized. It meant, definitely, a postponement of his plans for cashing the counterfeit bills he'd already made and for making more of them. It meant he'd have to stay poor a while longer. How long? He didn't know; it would depend on just how close the investigation got, whether even the slightest breeze of suspicion blew his way. If not—if the police came to see him only once and then didn't come again or check on him in other directions—then maybe a month or two would be long enough. If they seemed to suspect him even slightly, it might be a hell of a long time before he'd dare make a move. But there was no reason, damn it, why they should suspect him. What reason could they think he had for killing a man whom he'd met only once?

He wondered if his friend in the detective bureau, Charlie Barrett, would be assigned to the case. He hoped so. It would be easy to pump Charlie to keep in touch with the police investigation, to find out through Charlie whether the police accepted the crime as a casual robbery or were investigating it as a personally motivated murder.

And it certainly wouldn't seem unnatural to Charlie for him to be interested in the case after the police had once come to him about it. Any more than it had seemed unnatural to Charlie for him to be interested in the progress of the police in finding Myrtle's murderer. And Charlie knew about his interest in reading about crime and criminals, would probably think it odd if he wasn't interested in any case that touched him however distantly.

Yes, he'd have to look up Charlie again—he hadn't happened to see him for several months now—unless Charlie was the one who came to him to ask him about the car deal with Atkins. He hoped it would work out that way; it would seem more natural for him to keep on pumping Charlie afterwards.

He was crossing Olympic when he suddenly realized the mistake he had made. He should never have left the body and the car together—the car with its identifying registration and license number!

He should have rolled Atkins out of the car, back there in the dark and then driven the car somewhere else and left it where it might not be investigated for days, on some quiet side street without parking limitations. That way, since he'd left no identification on the body itself, it might be a day or two days before the police identified the body and not until they'd done that would they learn of the car swap and get to him, Conn.

Oh, it wasn't a fatal error, not necessarily even a dangerous one. (Unless the body and the car were found tonight instead of in the morning and the investigation got to him quickly before he was ready for it, unless police would be waiting for him when he got home tonight.) Just a mistake of omission but think of the extra time it would give him to make sure that he'd covered every angle, that not even a detailed search of house and shop would disclose anything that could lead to suspicion of counterfeiting or of murder.

He stopped, hesitating whether to turn back or to go on, then realized he was now nearer his own car and that it would be quicker for him to go to it and drive it back to within easy walking distance of where he'd left the convertible. Safer, too, because by driving past the mouth of the alley before he parked he could make sure that the body hadn't yet been found. There'd be lights, police cars, if it had been. And in that case he'd better drive home fast and work fast in case they got to him before morning.

A cab—but there wouldn't be one, of course, now that he really wanted one. He stepped out to the curb and saw that a cab was coming, empty. He flagged it down. Got in.

"Dock Street," he said. "just around the corner from Main. I don't know the exact address."

" 'Kay Mister. You mean the tavern there?"

"That's it," Conn said. Be safer that way, he thought, even if he lost a couple of minutes going into the tavern for a quick one, than to risk having the cab driver see him going to his own parked car, possibly noticing the make and model, wondering what the score was. He'd think nothing of a trip to a tavern.

"Sure a swell night for February, huh?" the driver asked him.

"Yeah. Sure."

Lincoln to Pico and west on Pico, now on the same route along which he'd followed Atkins a couple of hours ago. Main Street to Dock, and the turn.

"Okay, Mister. Fifty-five."

Conn got a single from his wallet. Wanted to save time by telling the driver to keep the change but decided he didn't want to make the driver remember him by either over-or-under-tipping. "Take out another quarter," he said.

" 'Kay, thanks."

In the doorway Conn stopped to light a cigarette, turning casually back to see if the cab was pulling away yet. But it was still parked there and the driver had turned on the dome light to enter the trip on his trip list card. Conn went on into the tavern.

Just as he'd left it, except that the liquor salesman was gone. But the same party of four was in the same booth, no one else in the place except the bartender. One of the women in the booth was laughing hysterically and one of the men was trying to shush her.

Conn slid onto a stool. "Just a nightcap," he said, "Whisky straight, little water on the side."

"Sure. What'd you do with the redhead?"

Conn grinned. "Chickened out on me. Oh well, I'm ready to turn in myself."

"What he gets for drinking doubles. Take it slow and you last longer."

From back in the booth a voice called out, "Hey, Jack. Four more the same way."

"Jesus God," the bartender said, looking at Conn. "All evening four drinks at a time, all different. One Manhattan, one old-fashioned, one martini, one daiquiri."

Conn grinned at him and as the bartender moved away, he reached for his drink. But he didn't down it right away. On second thought, he didn't want to call attention by being in too much of a hurry, and besides a few minutes couldn't matter; it would do him good to sit here a minute and plan calmly.

So he wouldn't overlook another bet.

Plan everything this time. Get in his car and drive over to Wilshire and past the mouth of the alley, making sure everything was quiet. Park a block or two beyond and walk back. Maybe walk around the block and into the alley from the other end? Yes, that would be safer. Much more chance of his being seen entering the alley from the Wilshire end than from the Arizona end. Pull or roll or push the body out of the convertible. Get into the car and back it into the alley. Drive out the Wilshire end because it would be headed that way. Don't turn on the lights until the car is out into the alley facing straight so they won't shine on the body.

Drive the car—oh, half a dozen blocks would be plenty, just so he put it on a side street without parking zone limitations. Walk back to his own car and drive home.

So damned simple; why hadn't he thought of it before? The car probably wouldn't be spotted till Monday—unless, well if the police got identification on Atkins sooner than that and had their prowl cars watching for Atkins' car, then it would be sooner. But not before tomorrow afternoon, even in that case.

Think. Think carefully. Was he overlooking anything, anything at all, this time? Have to do a good job of wiping off fingerprints this time, since they'd be on the wheel. But he wouldn't have overlooked that.

He sighed deeply. Was he calm enough now? Slightly under the edge of the bar, so the bartender wouldn't notice it, he held out his hand and watched to see if it was steady. It was.

He looked at his drink again and remembered he hadn't paid for it. He started an involuntary gesture toward his hip pocket for his wallet, and then stopped it. Why not pay for it out of Atkins' wallet and give himself a chance to make sure that all eight of the missing bills were in it? The two wallets were about the same size and both plain brown leather; the bartender wouldn't know or notice. And he knew that, besides the counterfeit tens, there was good money there too, the change out of the one bill Atkins had put on the bar.

Casually he took Atkins' wallet from the inside pocket of his coat, casually took out the top single and put it on the bar. Then, very casually, he opened it wider and started leafing through the other bills. As a man might do at the end of an evening's wandering to see how much money he'd spent and how much he had left.

Three singles, a five, another five, an old worn ten— and—God there couldn't be eight new tens there! At first he thought it was only two of them, then he counted with trembling fingers and made it three. Three, but only three.

Five bills, fifty dollars missing.

"Something the matter, Mister?" Bartender's voice.

"No." He guessed it was his own voice, although it sounded strange, stranger than the gimmicked dentures could account for. He realized that he was still staring into the wallet and quickly put it back in his pocket. Started to reach for his drink and then realized his hand would tremble violently if he tried to pick it up now and dropped his hands into his lap. Carefully looked at nothing.

"Jeez, *are* you all right? Look like you seen a ghost or something?"

"I'm all right," he said.

The bartender was putting the four diverse drinks on a tray. He took another look at Conn and then started around the bar toward the booth.

Be calm. Think.

Atkins could have, must have, paid a bill with that fifty dollars, somewhere between the printing shop and his girl's place. Or paid it to his landlady? Hardly that much for one week's room and board, but he might have been a week or two behind or—while he was flush—have paid for a week or two ahead.

Or maybe have left half of his money in his room when he'd stopped there to dress up for his date?

But, oh God, in *any* of those cases, five counterfeit bills together, paid out or put away together . . . In any of those cases they'd trace back to Atkins the minute the bills were in the hands of the police. Through Atkins to Conn.

A useless murder, a murder to no purpose. Except the cyanide chamber.

He wanted to laugh, but he made himself sit still, very still. Thank God the bartender was gone from behind the bar. Now he could reach for that drink and his trembling hand wouldn't matter. He bent forward over it as he lifted and spilled only a little.

Calm. Be calm and think.

Maybe there was still a way out. Besides running. Keep that in mind, he told himself to calm himself; *you can still run and have a chance.*

Think. Be calm. Everything would still be all right if there was some way he could find out where that fifty dollars had gone and get it back. Extra risk, sure, but what did extra risk matter? Now that he was sunk anyway, and for murder. Not just for counterfeiting and a life behind bars but for the big rap, for the cyanide egg.

What did he have to lose *now* in trying to burgle Atkins' room—except how did he know which room in that house was Atkins' room?

And then suddenly his mind was clicking again; he was thinking clearly and logically. There was an excellent chance that either Atkins had left the money in his room or had paid it out to his landlady. All he had to do was hold up the landlady—surely she herself and not a roomer would answer the door this late at night—she'd answered it before, hadn't she?—and rob her, make her tell him which room was Atkins'—

It would take improvisation, sure. Without knowing the layout, this pressed for time, he'd have to work things out as he went along. . . .

"Feeling better now?"

"I'm all right," Conn said. "Get a little twinge like that once in a while, but it doesn't mean anything. I had a checkup on it."

"Oh," the bartender said. "Yeah, you look okay now." He picked up the dollar from the bar, rang up the sale and put back a fifty cent piece in front of Conn.

"One more," Conn said. "Might as well kill the buck."

But he drank it quickly and left. No other customers seemed to be coming in and it would be a while before the party in the booth would order again. And he couldn't think clearly with the bartender staying right there in front of him, probably wanting to talk.

He went to his car and sat in it behind the wheel. Put the ignition key in the lock but didn't turn it yet. He had to think this out, make sure he was making no mistake, overlooking no reasonable possibility.

First and most important he should carry out his plan to get the body out of the car and the car where it wouldn't be found quickly. That was more important, much more important, now that his plans were being changed. It would give him more time and time was more important now than it had been. With the body and the car in different places and not together he could take time to watch the rooming house until all the lights were out and he'd have to deal with only the landlady, in whose room the bell would ring. Time to plan as many moves ahead as he could.

But he might as well get over the first hurdle first, before he planned farther. Every minute he waited increased the possibility, however slight it might be, of the car and the body being found together tonight, before he could separate them.

He reached for the ignition key but, just before he turned it, pulled his hand back. He *was* overlooking a bet.

He'd looked in the wallet only for money. The five tens weren't there, not even in one of the card compartments because none of them was fat enough to have held five folded bills. But one of the other compartments could contain a receipt for that fifty dollars or whatever part of it Atkins had paid out for a bill.

He reached across the car and turned on the dome light switch, took the wallet out of his pocket. He pulled out the driver's license and the few things under it. Social Security card. An automobile liability insurance company's identification card.

A small folded rectangle of paper. A woman's handwriting. A promissory note, dated this day, for the sum of fifty dollars and no cents.

Signed, Rose Harper.

Her name was Rose Harper and she was happy and unhappy at the same time. She was happy because she was deeply in love and she was unhappy because she couldn't sleep and it was midnight already. Midnight, three and a half hours after she'd got into bed at nine-thirty, and only four hours before she'd have to get up. That awful early shift. Why in heaven's name hadn't she told Mr. Howard she had other plans and couldn't make it? And if he'd insisted she could have quit right then and there over the telephone and never have had to go to the restaurant again except once to collect what pay she had coming. If only she'd done that she'd have the whole week end free for Claude instead of—unless she could get to sleep *somehow* she was going to be dead tired, a wreck with rings under her eyes, when he picked her up tomorrow afternoon and that would spoil everything.

She was going to quit that job anyway, wasn't she? It had been a mistake for her to have taken it, even though it did pay more money. She'd been greedy, that's what had been wrong with her. But six months ago—it had been just before she'd met Claude—those extra dollars per week seemed important. She'd had a pleasant easy-to-do bookkeeping job at bookkeeping and billing in the office of a Santa Monica department store; although she hadn't exactly enjoyed the work it hadn't been unpleasant and the hours had been regular. But it had paid only forty dollars a week and Alyce Randall, who had been a friend of hers then (although she'd lost touch with her a month afterwards when Alyce had moved to San Diego) had told her, "Honey, you're a sucker for that kind of dough. Be a waitress. With tips I'm making sixty sweet little dollars every week and you're smarter than I am any day." And Alyce had talked her into it and had shown her how, giving her private lessons for hours one week end so she could claim to have had experience and get away with it. And she'd got away with it, although she'd been a little awkward at first and had got a few bawlings-out from Mr. Howard before she'd really got the hang of it.

And she *was* making more money than she had at bookkeeping, although not as much as Alyce had predicted, not as much as some of the other girls were making on the same shifts. She was, by now, just about as efficient as any of them, but she was too shy; she just couldn't do the kind of kidding around with the customers some of the other girls did, the kind of kidding around that upped tips more than quiet and efficient service could ever hope to do. Still, she *was* making more than she had at the department store. Instead of sixty a week she'd been averaging a little less than fifty, but still about eight dollars a week more than she'd made at office work.

But it wasn't worth it. The work was harder physically and left her tired half the time, and the hours were not only longer but they weren't regular hours. As one of the newer girls—and one of the less brash ones when it came to arguing with the manager—she found herself getting the shifts the other girls didn't want, evenings, Saturdays, Sundays. It hadn't mattered too much at first, not until she had started going with Claude. He worked a regular Monday through Friday day shift and most of her time off was while he was working and vice versa. He'd complained plenty about it and she hadn't blamed him.

Yes, definitely, now that they were engaged, now that they were going to be married, she'd quit the waitress job and go back to office work, no matter how much less money she made. *Any* office job would do, just so the hours were regular. That was a lot more important than a few dollars a week difference in how much she made.

Why, oh *why* had she let the restaurant job spoil things tonight, tonight of all nights? Tonight when she had decided that Claude really loved her and really wanted to marry her and that she wouldn't keep him waiting any longer.

If only she hadn't said yes to Mr. Howard, Claude would be here with her right now, right at this very moment!

Instead, just because habit and weakness had made her say yes to the restaurant manager a few hours ago, here she was trying vainly to sleep on what should have been the most important night of her life. And instead gave every indication of being the longest night instead.

She just *had* to get to sleep, to get *some* sleep. . . .

The clock ticked. The clock that was set for four o'clock, only four hours from now. Less than that for it must have been at least ten minutes since she'd last looked at it.

She was less sleepy, more wide awake, than she'd ever been before. What if she hadn't slept at all when that clock went off?

If only she weren't so darned conscientious she'd just turn it off right now and, once she got to sleep, sleep as long as she could. What could Mr. Howard do but fire her? But she'd promised she'd be in at five and she would. Was it a strength or a weakness to be unable to break one's word? She'd been brought up that way, brought up strictly never to break a promise, and she just couldn't change now. Dependable, she thought bitterly, that's me, dependable. Deep-endable to the deep end.

Was it four hours now that she'd been lying here sleepless? Was it half past twelve yet? She did and didn't want to know.

Did she dare, she wondered, move the alarm fifteen minutes ahead and sleep (if she slept at all) until a quarter after four? It took her only half an hour to get to work; could she be ready in fifteen minutes? She thought she could. She'd bathed already, after Claude had left (and had seen her body with new and wondering eyes in view of what was so soon to happen)—yes, she could do it. No time for toast and coffee but sleep was more important.

Enough light came in the window for her to see to change the alarm clock setting. It was twelve-fifteen now so she still had four hours. She sat up in bed to shake down the pillow and then lay down again telling herself resolutely, *sleep, darn you, sleep. Don't think, just go to sleep.*

And wondered what Claude was doing. He probably hadn't gone right home and to bed, leaving so early, but probably he was home by now. Was he sleeping, if he *was* home, or was he lying awake thinking about her as she was thinking about him, thinking about tomorrow?

Why, oh why, while there was still time, just after Mr. Howard's phone call, hadn't he talked her into calling back and changing her yes into a no, quitting right then so they'd have had the whole week end, starting right then?

He could have talked her into it and everything would have been perfect. Why hadn't he?

Don't blame Claude, she told herself; it was your own fault because of that little white lie you told him about there being "another reason" why tomorrow would be better;

you knew perfectly well how he would understand that and you knew that his understanding it that way would keep him from arguing tonight. You told him a lie and you know it. Not literally a lie, of course, because there was another reason but it was just that you were still a little frightened; you wanted another day before it happened. But it was a lie just the same because you knew Claude would think you meant something else.

And if you hadn't told that lie he would probably be here with you right now and you wouldn't be going through all of this, trying to sleep with a deadline so soon ahead and a hard day's work beyond the deadline.

Once you'd made up your mind to give yourself to him why didn't you have the courage to do it then instead of postponing, waiting?

The phone rang.

She scrambled out of bed and without wasting time trying to find the light switch she groped her way across the room in the almost dark, almost falling over a chair but hardly noticing it.

It must be Claude! Or news about Claude?

Had he had a few drinks and decided to call her to see if he could change her mind about tonight? Had it come to him as it had come to her that she didn't have to go to work tomorrow, that she was quitting her job anyway? Or had he had an accident and were the police or someone calling to tell her about it? Please, God, let it be Claude and not bad news about him. And if it was she'd tell him yes to come, to come right away. Even if his voice was a little fuzzy with drink; she wouldn't care about that, not tonight. Oh, let it be that. She'd seen Claude before when he'd drunk a little too much and he was just a little amusing that way and just a little pathetic, never objectionable. And while she waited for him she'd catch up a little by drinking some more of the wine in the refrigerator quickly so they'd both be a little—

"Hello," she said breathlessly. "Claude?"

"I beg your pardon." It was a man's voice, an unfamiliar voice. "Is this Pico 4-8232?"

The letdown made her want to laugh hysterically, but she kept her voice level. No, it's 8223, not 8232."

"Oh, sorry. I must have dialed it wrong. Hope I didn't disturb you."

She said, "That's all right," and put down the receiver. And sat there quietly until her heart quit pounding quite so hard. She ought, she knew, to be *mad* but she was too disappointed and upset to work up anger. At least against anyone other than herself for having been so foolish in jumping to a conclusion.

A full minute she sat there in the dark and then she sighed and stood up. She knew it would be futile to go back to bed right away so she turned on the light instead. Maybe a glass of warm milk would help; it was supposed to help, anyway.

She got the carton of milk from the refrigerator and poured some of it into a saucepan to warm on the stove. Stood watching it so it wouldn't boil.

Shivered a little and realized that the room was quite cool and that she was barefoot and dressed only in thin pajamas. She went to the closet for robe and slippers and when she got back to the stove the milk hadn't boiled yet but looked as though it was warm enough. She poured it into a thick glass and took it over to the table, sat down and began to sip it.

Her handbag was lying there on the table in front of her and she remembered that it held the fifty dollars—the five new ten dollar bills—Claude had left for her to put into her bank account to save for him. She'd put the bills in her purse while she was straightening up after he had left.

But she remembered now that tomorrow—today, rather —was Saturday and that she wouldn't be able to go to the bank until at least Monday; she didn't want to carry the money with her all that time. Maybe she should hide it away somewhere now, especially since, now that she'd reset the alarm clock, she'd be in pretty much of a hurry in the morning.

The shoe box in the closet where she kept a few other valuable or personal things, with tissue paper over them and a pair of shoes on top? Yes, probably that was the best hiding place for money too, until she could take it to the bank.

She got the box from the closet, sat down at the table again and took another sip of the warm milk before she opened it. Then she took out the shoes, shoes that she never wore because they hurt her feet but they were too good to throw away. (Someday her feet might shrink?) And the tissue paper. In the bottom of the box lay her insurance policy for two thousand dollars, a twenty-year endowment with sixteen years to go; birth certificate, dated twenty-three years ago, certificates of graduation from high school and from business school, and, with a rubber band around them in lieu of a blue ribbon, the letters Claude had written her last month, all three of them. The three letters he'd written her during the ten days she'd been upstate in Sacramento when her sister was in the hospital, dangerously sick. That had been a bad week and a half until the last day or so when she'd known that Elsie was out of danger and wouldn't die after all. A bad week and a half except for the three high points of those three letters he'd written her.

She'd been in love with him already, then, had been for two or three months, although she hadn't dared let him guess how *much* she was in love with him, because he might not really have been in love with her. Oh, he *said* he was, but he hadn't said anything about marriage, even remotely, except in a negative way by letting her know in one subtle way or another how much he prized being free and single. It must have been during that absence from one another that Claude had started thinking about marrying her, although he hadn't actually proposed until last Sunday, two weeks after she was back. At any rate he'd found out that he missed her.

The letters proved that, and the fact that there'd been three of them in so short a time.

Only she'd loved him so much that she hadn't dared let herself *believe* those letters because then she would have been really overboard, ready to be hurt horribly if the wrong side won in the battle that was going on inside Claude—the battle between his love for her and his love for freedom and bachelorhood. That battle had been a hard one, she knew.

She too had had a hard battle with herself but the lines had been differently drawn there. It had been a fight to keep herself from loving him *too* much and giving in to him, until and unless he won his battle, until and unless she knew she could let go and love him with her heart and her body both, without reservation, and without heartbreak at the end of it.

Thank you, God, that both battles are over now.

But why, why, *why* had she let him go tonight?

Tomorrow seemed ages away, and what if something happened to him, or to her before then? She told herself, don't be silly; nothing like that will happen. But what if it did?

His handwriting on the top envelope, such straight and strong and masculine handwriting, so much like Claude himself. Not pretty but firm and legible, with character in it. She'd never thought much about graphology, but maybe there was something in it. Was she herself like her own handwriting? A thought came to her: If there really was anything in graphology, then her handwriting should be different after tomorrow, because she herself would be different. Was different now, for that matter.

She picked up the three envelopes and took the rubber band from around them, took out the first letter to read it lovingly. She could reread these letters now with more pleasure than when she'd read them first because now she didn't have to worry, now she knew that Claude meant everything in them—meant it now even if he'd still been doubtful or had had reservations at the time he'd written them.

Honey:

I miss you like hell. Guess I had to have you away to find out how much I love you, how crazy I am about you . . .

Her eyes misted a little. But, darn it, she *shouldn't* be reading these now. She had to get to sleep and the more she thought about Claude the less chance she had. But none of the letters was long and she read all three of them before she put them back in the shoe box. She put the fifty dollars and the other things back in, and put the shoe box back in the closet.

She drank the rest of the milk and rinsed out the glass.

A quarter of one. Only three and a half hours now before that alarm clock would go off like a little bomb. Would she get any sleep at *all*?

Well, if she hadn't she just wouldn't go to work. Because then she could phone the restaurant and tell them she was sick and wasn't coming in, either for that early shift or for the later one she'd originally been scheduled to work, and it wouldn't be a lie, or not much of a lie because if she went to work without any sleep at all she'd be making herself sick before the day was over. And spotting everything for Claude and herself.

Why didn't she decide right now that she wasn't going in? Why was she being so conscientious about a job she was going to give up anyway? Had they been specially nice to her? Not that she'd noticed. Except about her going to Sacramento last month; Mr. Howard had "held her job" for her; but that had been because he was short of waitresses and needed her back. And of course she'd have quit and gone anyway if he had told her she couldn't take off; he probably knew that.

All right, then, she just wouldn't go to work tomorrow, either shift. She'd just phone at five when the restaurant opened and tell them she was sick and didn't know when she was coming in. And Monday she'd go in and quit officially, collect the six days pay she had coming through Friday, and start looking for an office job again.

She sighed with relief now that the decision had been made, now that she wouldn't have to get up early, except briefly to make the phone call and let them know she wasn't coming in.

And sometime later in the morning—maybe she'd better reset the alarm for about ten o'clock after it had gone off at five—she'd have to phone Claude at the rooming house. To let him know to come here instead of driving to the restaurant.

And now that she didn't *have* to sleep, she probably would be able to. And if she *could* get to sleep right away—

No, she wasn't going to let her conscience spoil things for her again. She *wasn't* going to work tomorrow, no matter what.

Firmly she marched over to the alarm clock and changed its setting a second time, to five o'clock. Too bad she'd have to interrupt her sleep, however briefly, after four hours but that couldn't be helped. If she didn't phone them they'd phone her to find out whether she was coming, and that would be as bad; worse, because telling them then would lead to more argument.

She put robe and slippers back in the closet and then stood, looking around a moment, wondering if there was anything else she should do, this time, before getting back into bed.

Caught sight of her pajama-clad reflection in the mirror over the bureau, a slender brown-haired reflection that regarded her as gravely as she regarded it, until suddenly they both smiled. Both thinking about Claude and tomorrow, both regretting Claude and tonight. Both thinking, if only the phone call hadn't been a wrong number, if it had only been Claude wanting to come back—

Then she flicked the light switch and the reflection wasn't there any longer.

The room seemed darker than it had been before and she looked around, wondering why. Then she saw that it was because the light outside in the hallway had gone out; the transom had been open a few inches at the top for ventilation and a streak of light had come in. But it didn't matter; her eyes were quickly adapting themselves to the dark. She could see the white rectangle of the bed across the room and took a step toward it.

Stopped suddenly because she thought she heard a sound from the door. Thought but wasn't sure. Then the sound came again and she was sure. Not a knock but a soft tapping, as of fingertips. And again, just a little louder.

She took the two steps that brought her to the door, not quite believing, not quite daring to believe. Very quietly, very breathlessly, she asked, "Who is it?" Almost in a whisper.

Her answer *was* a whisper. "It's me, Claude, honey. Open the—"

But she was already opening the door.

His name was John Dubinski, Conn said. He spelled out the last name carefully for the clerk at the storage company in Manhattan Beach. "D-u-b-i-n-s-k-i."

"And your address?" the clerk asked him.

He wouldn't have an address for a while, Conn explained. He'd be traveling for several months and no, there wasn't any address he could use as a "permanent" address meanwhile. He didn't even know whether, when he wanted the two suitcases again, he'd be near enough to pick them up himself or whether he'd have to write to have them shipped to him. They could be shipped to him collect, couldn't they, if he needed them?

"Sure," the clerk said. "I mean, the shipping charges can be collect, if you're paid up to then on the storage charges. They got to be paid in advance."

"Okay." Conn took out his wallet. "I'll pay the storage for six months ahead now. If I haven't called for them or sent for them by then, I'll send in more money from wherever I am. You won't have an address to send me a notice to, but I'll keep track of the date." He put a bill on the counter.

The clerk nodded, gave Conn his change and a receipt.

"Oh, one other thing," Conn said. "I'll be around town a few days maybe, before I take off. I just might decide there are a couple of other items I'd like to put in one of the suitcases, things I decide I don't want to carry with me. That'll be okay, won't it?"

"Long as you don't run it over a hundred pounds. That's the minimum and that's what I'm charging you for. If you run it over a hundred, the rate'll go up. But those weigh only seventy together so you wouldn't be likely to add enough to send 'em over. Bring that receipt if you come in."

"Right. Thanks," Conn said.

Outside, he walked the block over to Highland where he'd left his car. Drove along slowly until he saw a mailbox and stopped. He had the envelope ready. Return address, John Dubinski, Gen. Del., Manhattan Beach, Calif. Ready to be mailed to: Mr. Dean Bratten, Gen. Del., Venice, Calif. The key to his bank deposit vault was already in the envelope, in a folded piece of paper. He added the receipt from the storage company and sealed the envelope carefully. He got out of the car and mailed it.

Back in the car and heading toward Santa Monica again, he sighed with relief.

That was it. He'd done absolutely everything he could do until Monday when the bank would be open again.

The counterfeit money and the plates in that safe deposit box—in his own name, in his own bank—were, as of this moment the only things that could possibly link him either to counterfeiting or to murder.

Everything else was taken care of. He'd had the whole night from one o'clock on, to check and recheck every possibility. To check and recheck himself, his house, his car, the shop. There was nothing in his possession, not the tiniest scrap of paper or drop of ink or blood (there had been no blood in either murder) that might incriminate him in any way.

Nothing but the money and plates in the deposit box. Damn, if this were only a weekday instead of Saturday, he could have taken care of that too. But it wasn't, and after all it entailed only a very slight risk. If the police suspected him at all (and why should they?) it certainly wouldn't be to the extent that they'd immediately check with his bank, find out he had a deposit box and get a court order to open it.

After Monday morning they could check and be damned. Monday morning he'd drive to Venice and pick up that envelope John Dubinski had mailed to Dean Bratten as soon as the general delivery window opened. From there to the bank to get the plates and the money (and leave in lieu of them other papers, deeds and policies and what not, to account for his having had need of a box). From the bank to Manhattan Beach where he would make the addition to the contents of one of the suitcases.

After that he could again put the key to the safe deposit box on the ring with his other keys.

And there would remain only one loose end, the receipt from the storage company. He'd have to keep that, of course. Or at least keep track of it. But it was such a tiny thing that surely, over the week end while it was in the mail, he'd think of some absolutely safe place to keep it so even the most thorough search couldn't turn it up. Or if there was suspicion of him and any real likelihood of a search being made, he could always keep remailing it to himself via general delivery once a week until things had blown over or until he'd figured out a safe place for it.

He was probably being overcareful about the whole thing. There was absolutely no connection that the police could find between Conn and Atkins except the perfectly innocent fact that they'd traded cars. And he could tell them the truth about that. There was even less connection that the police could find between Conn and the Harper girl. The only danger he'd run was the danger of something having gone wrong during one of the killings, of being caught red-handed. And that danger was past.

He'd been driving slowly but he put his foot a little harder on the accelerator when he remembered that it was after nine o'clock now. The police would have found Atkins hours ago and just possibly by now they would have identified him and have started the round of questioning his friends and acquaintances, people he'd worked with or done business with.

And it would be better for him to be home so he wouldn't have to lie about where he'd just been and what he'd just been doing. Every lie you had to tell was an additional danger, however slight a one.

Let's see, if by any chance there would be a detective waiting when he got home, did he have a plausible and not disprovable story of where he had been? He worked one out and, not too near home or too far from it, stopped at a grocery store for a few purchases to implement it.

But no one was waiting for him.

There was still coffee on the stove from the breakfast he'd made for himself a few hours before, after he'd finished the packing and was waiting until it was late enough for storage companies to be open for business. He turned the fire on under it to heat it again. He'd have to keep going today on coffee and nerve until after the police had been around to talk to him.

God, how he wanted to sleep. But if they found him sleeping when they came, that wouldn't be good. It might make them wonder what he'd been doing the night before.

And he didn't want them to wonder.

Not that he was worried now about them being able to prove anything against him, but if they even suspected him in the slightest degree, then the big plan, the counterfeiting, would have to be postponed for a long time. If he were seriously suspected, it might have to be abandoned completely. He'd just have to wait his chance to get the suitcases out of storage and dispose of their contents permanently. A year's work wasted. And stuck back in the old dull futureless rut.

Or would it be quite the same? Even though he could never tell anyone, could never brag about it, he'd have the secret knowledge that he'd committed and got away with not one but three perfect crimes. Three perfect murders. No matter what he seemed to others, he'd have that secret knowledge, that secret satisfaction in his own cleverness. An even greater satisfaction in a way if the police suspected him of two of those murders but found themselves unable to match his cleverness by proving what they suspected.

And how, short of getting hold of those two suitcases, which were at least temporarily safe, could they possibly convict him of murder? Even if they suspected him of counterfeiting (and once he'd taken care of the safe deposit box, they could do no more than suspect him) how could they deduce therefrom any motive he could have had for killing Rose Harper? His reason for killing Atkins, yes, they might guess that. But no one now alive would know that Atkins had lent his fiancée that fifty dollars.

But no matter what they suspected, what could they *prove?*

No one who had seen him with Atkins would be able to make positive identification, and not many people had even seen them together. Of course there was Atkins' landlady. She'd tell the police that a man answering the description she'd give them had inquired for Atkins early in the evening and had looked up Rose Harper's address in her telephone book. And the bartender in the tavern on Dock Street had seen them together. But that was all, and it wouldn't get them anywhere.

Just the same, drinking coffee now, he ran over it again, making sure he'd made no mistakes.

After he'd left the tavern the second time he'd first carried out his plan to get Atkins' body out of the car and then move the car so that, with the body one place and the car another, identification of the body wouldn't be immediate and automatic.

Then taking care of Rose Harper had been easy. He'd phoned, pretending to get a wrong number, to make sure that she was home; it had occurred to him that just possibly she worked a night shift at one of the airplane factories or somewhere, which would have accounted for Atkins' having left so early. And he had another reason for making the call; if she was home it would be better if she wasn't too soundly asleep. He knew he'd have to knock and pretend to be Atkins, and he didn't want to have to knock loudly enough to waken any of the neighbors too. He'd made the call from the tavern a block from her place on Pico, the tavern from which he'd already phoned her once earlier in the evening. But the second time, in the privacy of the telephone cubicle in the hallway, he'd taken out his dentures while he made the call. It made his voice sound different and he didn't want her to connect the wrong number with the earlier call and become suspicious.

After the call he'd finished his drink and then had gone to the building and upstairs. It had surprised him to see the crack of light over the transom of her door. But it was so late by then and the building was so quiet he felt pretty sure that everyone in the other apartments was home and asleep so it would be safe for him to wait a while to see if her light went out soon. And while he was waiting he'd turned off the hallway light. Nothing to lose by doing that and plenty to gain if she opened her door with her own room in darkness—as she might if she thought it was her fiancé come back.

And she'd made it easy for him by doing just that. He'd been able to strike before she could realize that he wasn't Atkins, and she'd never known what hit her. If she had turned her own light back on before opening the door he'd have been ready, the weapon already raised, and felt sure he could have struck quickly enough, before she could have screamed.

But it was better as it happened, especially for the girl. She had died, as Atkins had died, without warning. Suddenly and unexpectedly and without knowing that she was being killed, spared even a fraction of a second of terror before oblivion. Yes, it made him feel better, much better, that he'd been able to do that much for both of them. Their deaths had been even more merciful than Myrtle's; she had been unconscious while he had strangled her, but she had had a fractional second of knowledge that he was going to strike and hurt her before the blow had landed. Neither Atkins nor the Harper girl had had even that.

He'd been able to step forward and catch her to let her down easily; there hadn't even been a thud. So he'd been able to take his time searching for the money and it was a good thing that he had been able to; the money had been well hidden.

It would have been better, in a way, for him to have confused the issue by leaving her place just as he had found it, her other money safely in her purse and no evidence that anything had been taken. But it had been too rough a job finding the money; by the time he got to it, the fact that a search had been made was obvious. And he'd been handicapped too by having to avoid leaving fingerprints, working for the first fifteen or twenty minutes with a handkerchief wrapped loosely around each hand until he'd been lucky enough to come across a pair of white cotton work gloves big enough for him to put on. So he'd gone to the opposite extreme by making it even more obvious that the entire place had been ransacked and by taking the money from her purse, the few pieces of inexpensive jewelry he found, and the other papers and the letters to her from Atkins that he had found in the shoe box with the real object of his search.

He didn't leave until he was absolutely sure he was leaving no possible clue behind him. He remembered, going out through the hallway, to turn on the light behind him, and to wipe off the switch.

Then home and to work, *really* to work. Making sure that he got *everything*, every vestige of every disguise, every scrap of paper, everything he'd taken off Atkins and from the girl's room, the gun, the works. Some of the things could have been burned, but since it couldn't all be burned, he was smart enough not to try burning any of it. Burning leaves ashes and what do you do with ashes in a house which is heated only by gas grates? No matter how careful you are, even if you think you flush every vestige of ash down the toilet, there will remain somehow evidence that something has been burned. Even if it's only a smell that might cling for days.

A few things could be taken back to the printing shop, things that had come from there originally, engraving tools and the hand press. Things that wouldn't be out of place in the shop but that should never be found at the house.

Everything else fitted easily into the two suitcases.

A long job, but he'd finished (and checked and rechecked) while it was still too early for him to risk going to the shop and much too early to find a storage company open. He'd made himself breakfast, and then had made his trip to the shop at half past seven, early enough that none of the adjacent shops was open but not early enough to attract attention by having to turn on a light.

Then to Manhattan Beach, a half hour's drive away, to wait until a storage company had opened.

The mailing of the storage company's receipt and the bank deposit box key to a general delivery address nearby but not the Santa Monica post office, where some of the clerks might recognize him.

No, he'd made no mistake anywhere. Had left nothing undone.

Not just luck, either, as some might say his getting away with his wife's murder had been. Things had gone wrong several times, but he'd always been able to get around them, to improvise. Atkins having left the girl's place too early by only minutes and spoiling his original plan. The fact that only three of the eight bills still as of then to be accounted for had been in Atkins' wallet, which made him have to kill two people instead of one.

Two murders instead of one, and both of them perfect crimes. Perfect in every detail. Three, counting Myrtle.

He poured himself another cup of coffee and carried it into the living room where he could sit more comfortably. Took the easy chair within reach of the bookcase that held his books on true crimes and criminals. Glanced at the two favorites he'd read several times each—FAMOUS UNSOLVED CRIMES by Grantham and MURDERERS ANONYMOUS by Brady—but he didn't reach for one of them. For the moment, he was content to sit and think, feeling no need for the anodyne of the printed page. Especially as a warming thought had come to him.

Perhaps, although *his* name, he hoped, would never become the immortal name of a famous murderer, the crimes he had committed last night might easily become famous crimes, famous unsolved murders that might be written about over and over and remembered for generations or centuries.

Why not? Didn't they have all the classic elements to become famous? A young man and his fiancée both murdered on the same night, not together, but obviously by the same weapon in the same hand. A mysterious stranger who had inquired for the young man at his boarding house and who had learned where he was would be the obvious suspect—but he would never be found or identified. No one, no one at all would be found who would have any reasonable motive for killing both of them in separate crimes. Robbery would never hold water as the real motive. A former suitor of the girl's who had killed her and his successful rival?

That would be one of a hundred theories and possibilities, all wide of the mark. It could easily become a famous and forever mysterious double murder, one that would be written about over and over in books, magazines and Sunday supplements.

He was getting sleepy again, but he couldn't drink any more coffee; he was drowning in the stuff now. He took the cup out to the kitchen, came back and sat down again, reached for a book to help keep himself awake with, and then pulled back his hand.

Why shouldn't he let himself doze off? As long as he did so fully dressed and sitting up, what could it matter? He was a light sleeper; even dead tired as he was the doorbell would waken him easily.

He put his head back, sighed, relaxed, slept.

He was in a tavern arguing with Henry Jennings, the bank teller. Jennings was drunk, but he was sober. He wanted to break away, to go home to Myrtle, and Jennings was trying to talk him into picking up two women who were sitting at a corner table. He loved Myrtle and wanted Myrtle, not some other woman, but Jennings (who seemed to be his father as well as just Jennings) kept telling him that Myrtle wasn't good for him, that anyway if he went home she wouldn't let him have her because she didn't love him, and that he might as well settle for something he could have. "And it won't cost you anything," Jennings said. "It's on the lodge. It's all on the lodge." And Conn looked around and saw that the lodge meeting was being held right in the tavern, that he'd gone to the lodge meeting after all. The keeper of the Royal Tiger, which was the highest office in the chapter, was behind the bar in full lodge regalia, serving the drinks. He slid a drink to Conn and leered, making an obscene gesture as he pointed to the girls in the corner. "Printer's ink," he said cryptically. (Or had it been "Printer sink"?)

And they were all looking at Conn now and reciting the lodge oath of inward brotherhood, so he *had* to go now, over to the corner table and make the pickup for himself and Jennings. He didn't want to, but he *had* to. His father Jennings clapped him on the shoulder and then leaned over and whispered the lodge password into his ear.

Then gave him a shove toward the corner and he weaved his way through the crowd, in and among and around tables to the corner table where the girls sat. The one across the table, watching him, was a pretty brunette; the one with her back toward him was a blonde, her hair the color of Myrtle's. The brunette looked at him as he approached. Her eyes got nasty and her mouth twisted; "Printer stink," it said clearly. The hell with her, Conn thought; Jennings could have her. He'd take the blonde with hair like Myrtle's. He came up behind her, touched her shoulder lightly.

She sprang up and turned to face him; it *was* Myrtle. They'd played a joke on him or something. But she was glaring hatred at him. She threw off her coat and she was naked, stark naked, standing there yelling at him, telling him viciously that he wasn't a *man,* that he was no good, no *damn* good—

The horrible thing was that *he* was naked too; he suddenly realized he didn't have anything on at all, and that the whole tavern, the whole lodge, had turned and was watching him and laughing. Laughing so loudly that he could no longer hear what Myrtle was saying. He turned and ran, *ran.*

Waves of laughter pushed him out into the night and he was in his car driving.

Laughter still ringing in his ears, driving south on Lincoln Boulevard, toward Manhattan Beach. There was something in Manhattan Beach he had to get; it was something important, something terribly important. But the road was slippery, his car—it was the yellow convertible—kept sliding from side to side, barely missing other cars. And finally it slid sidewise off the road and up against a low stone wall that bounded a cemetery. He could see over the wall, could see the graves and the white headstones. And something was trying to pull him out of the car and over the cemetery wall, something he couldn't see. Something that didn't want him to get to Manhattan Beach and safety, something that wanted to keep him here.

He was screaming as he fought his way out of the car,

screaming as he kicked his ankles free of something and ran, ran down the road into the night. From the cemetery behind him there was laughter, the same laughter there had been in the tavern, the same voices.

And the storage company, and he was handing a little white slip of paper across to the clerk behind the counter and the clerk was saying, "Yes, Mr. Dubinski; yes, Mr. D-u-b-i-n-s-k-i." "Yes, get it quickly," he said. "What is the article you are claiming, Mr. Dubinski?" And Dubinski-Conn said, "I don't know, but get it quickly, get it quickly please." The clerk said, "All right, Mr. Dubinski, I'll get it." Then the clerk disappeared.

And the clerk was back, dressed as an Episcopalian minister and he was holding Myrtle in his arms. Myrtle dead and stark naked, with her tongue protruding. The minister-clerk held Myrtle out to him. He said, "Do you take this woman as—?"

A bell was ringing. It pulled Conn back out of the dream, made him shake his head to clear it. *Jesus*, what a dream.

The doorbell meant the police were here. He shook his head again and stood up. He had to get his mind clear, and quickly.

Then the bell rang again and now he was awake enough to realize that it was the telephone bell and not the doorbell.

Things fell into place and he was awake as he walked over and picked up the phone. "Hello," he said. "Darius Conn speaking."

A man's smooth voice. "May I speak to Mrs. Conn please?"

"What?" He didn't believe he'd heard right.

"Mrs. Myrtle Conn, please. Is she there?"

"No. Who is this?"

"Carter Furriers, Mr. Conn, on Wilshire Boulevard. Mrs. Conn bought a cape here two years ago."

"What about it?" Yes, he remembered that cape all right. The fight Myrtle had put up to get it. The long months it had taken him to pay for it.

"A great many of our customers who have capes, Mr. Conn, are having them made over into stoles for spring. And this month we are making a special offer on making such an alteration. If Mrs. Conn would be interested—"

"Mrs. Conn would not be interested," Conn cut in. "She died a year ago."

"Oh. I'm very sorry to have bothered you, Mr.—"

Conn hung up the phone.

Went back to the chair again and sat down. What a lousy time to get a phone call asking for Myrtle. A full year after. He'd had calls asking for her several times in the first few weeks, even months, after her death, calls from shops or people who knew her slightly and apparently hadn't read of the murder.

He'd found such calls mildly annoying but none of them had given him the sudden shock this one had. But that was probably because it had been so long since such a thing had happened that he'd forgotten that it could happen. Or had it been because he'd been dreaming about Myrtle when he'd been awakened by the phone? He had been dreaming about her, but now he couldn't remember what the dream had been. Except that he remembered thinking, *Jesus, what a dream*, while he had still remembered at least a part of it.

It didn't matter. Dreams don't mean anything. Thank God he wasn't superstitious as Myrtle had been. Always buying astrology horoscopes, checking to see whether today was going to be a lucky day for her or an unlucky one. Had she checked her horoscope for the last day of her life, he wondered; and if so, what had it told her?

But bad luck hadn't been Myrtle's downfall; it had been her own viciousness and bad judgment. Chance (from her point of view) had made him come home too early. But he wouldn't have laid a hand on her except for her own words and actions, the intolerable things she said to him and the intolerable thing she did in flaunting her body before him, violated but by him inviolable. Stupid of her not to guess that she might be pushing him past a breaking point.

Superstition and luck were a lot of crap. Sure you got good breaks and bad breaks, but it was what you did with them that mattered. You had to take advantage of the good ones and be smart enough to change your plans and to improvise if you got a bad one.

He lighted a cigarette and then looked at his watch. It surprised him to see that it was almost noon. He must have slept about two hours before the telephone had wakened him.

He wondered whether to fix himself some lunch in the kitchen or to go out to a restaurant, decided that fresh air and driving a few blocks would do him good. Besides, he could pick up a paper and see if the story had broken yet.

It hadn't, in either of the two morning papers he picked up outside the restaurant and looked through while he ate. That didn't mean, of course, that Atkins' body hadn't been found. It must have been, hours ago. But it couldn't have been identified by the time these papers had gone to press or the story would have rated at least a short item. It wouldn't be a big story, of course, until the girl had been found too and the two murders linked together. Or, more likely, they wouldn't really have to be linked; the Harper girl would be found dead when they went to look her up as Atkins' fiancée after they'd identified him. Even then they'd think nothing when, the first time or two, she didn't answer her door or her telephone. Unless she was missed elsewhere. . . .

He left the two papers behind him in the restaurant.

Home was as he'd left it. He wandered around the house a while, wondering what to do with himself. He wasn't sleepy now and decided he could stick it through until a reasonable time for him to go to bed tonight without doing any more napping.

But he was too keyed up to read. Damn it, why didn't they come now and get it over with so he could relax. He wasn't worried, but he felt tense and a little excited.

But he killed time doing little chores around the house and a spot of house cleaning. (He was a much better house-keeper than Myrtle had ever been.) The afternoon passed somehow.

It was a few minutes after five o'clock when the doorbell finally rang.

He opened the door, then pulled it wide open. It was Charlie Barrett and he was alone. "Hi, Charlie. Come in."

Charlie gave him back the grin. "Long time no see, Darry. All right, I'll come in, but just for a minute. This is business, police business."

They went into the living room and sat down. Charlie tossed his panama onto the coffee table.

Conn said, "Charlie, you mean you've got a lead finally on—?"

Charlie Barrett's slightly balding head shook regretfully. "Sorry, no. Nothing on that. Darry, you know a Claude Atkins?"

"Claude Atkins? Yeah. That is, I met him once, couple of evenings ago. We swapped cars."

"As suddenly as that? How come?"

"I guess it was a little spur-of-the-moment for both of us, but it just happened that way. Say—there's no trouble about the car, is there? I mean, he didn't swap me a stolen job or anything like that, did he?"

"No, nothing like that. Atkins got himself killed last night, him and his girl friend both. No lead yet, we're just checking everybody who knew or had business with either of them, that's all. And in his room we found the registration slip on your car, signed over to him. So that's all. Just want to know what you can tell us about him or about the deal between you."

"Sure. Not that there's much to tell. How'd you go for a beer? I got some cans in the refrigerator."

"I'd better—oh hell, why not? I don't drink on duty but this is my last stop before dinner so it can't make any difference."

Conn went to the refrigerator and came back with a can of beer for each of them. He sat down and put his legs up over the arm of the chair.

"Night before last," he said. "Thursday evening. I met the guy in a tavern on Lincoln in Venice, across the street from the Lido Theater. Know where that is?"

Charlie Barrett nodded. "About what time?"

"Early in the evening, around seven. I'd intended originally to go to the movie there. I'd driven past the Lido the day before and an Alec Guinness picture was playing there. I thought it would probably still be on Thursday so I took a chance and drove over. But they'd changed pictures, to some damn western. So that's how I happened to go into the tavern, decided I might as well have a drink while I was out. And that's how I know it was seven o'clock, because I'd planned to make the first show.

"This Atkins was the only other guy at the bar and we got to talking. About the weather first, I guess. And then somehow about cars. He said something about being crazy to get a convertible and I told him he must be a little crazy already to want one, that I had one and wished to hell I had a coupe or a sedan, either one, instead of it. That damn yellow convertible, Charlie, I got just to please Myrtle; you remember that."

"Yeah."

"Well he asked me what year my convertible was and when I told him a forty-one, he got interested. He said his sedan was the same year and what was wrong with swapping, and did I have my car with me? His was parked right outside.

"I told him mine was too and we might as well look them over. So we finished the drinks we had—our first ones, or mine was my first anyway—and went outside to look over each other's cars. The convertible first. He backtracked right away about trading even, especially after he'd listened to the engine run. After I saw his boat, though, and tried it, I didn't blame him. He had it in top shape and it purred like a kitten and mine—well, it needed plenty of work to be in the shape his was. His rubber was better too.

"So we went back in the tavern and talked it over a while. Had one more drink apiece. Didn't have to dicker much; he wanted a hundred bucks difference and I offered seventy-five, and we called it off for ninety. I think I got a good deal. Say, Charlie, you want to take a look at the new boat?"

Charlie said, "Sure. I was going to suggest it, for another reason. He didn't leave any papers in the glove compartment, or anything in the trunk or anywhere, did he?" He stood up.

Conn said, "No, I looked it over. Sit down till you finish your beer. The car isn't going to run away. Well, that's all there is to tell you, I guess."

Charlie grunted and sat down again. "That's all you talked about? Weather and cars?"

"All I can remember. Why would that matter?"

"Just that you might tell us something that would give us a lead, that's all. For example, now take this tavern across from the Lido where you met him. Did he hang out there, do you think, or did he just happen to drop in like you did?"

Conn considered. "Damned if I know. He didn't say anything that'd show one way or the other— Wait, I do remember something. He had to go to the john once and had to ask the bartender where it was. There was a sign, but it didn't show from where we were sitting. So he couldn't have gone there regular."

Charlie laughed. "You ought to be a detective, Darry. Well, we'll check the place anyway and show his picture to the bartenders. He didn't mention any names of friends, anything like that?"

Conn shook his head. "No. Didn't even mention where he worked. Said be was a mechanic, though, unless I already said that. That came out while we were talking cars."

"Ever hear of a woman named Rose Harper?"

"No. Was that his girl friend, the one you said got killed with him?"

"Yeah, lived over on Pico. You're sure that's the only time you ever saw Atkins or talked to him?"

"Positive."

Charlie sighed. "Well, I guess that's it. Hell, if you're sure you looked in the glove compartment and the luggage compartment, there's no use me looking over the car too."

"I did and Atkins did," Conn said. "We signed over our registration papers and traded keys right in the tavern. But then when we went outside and before we drove off we both looked over both cars to be sure we weren't leaving any personal stuff in them."

"That's good enough. Well, I'd better—"

"Hey, wait a minute. I want to know what this is all about. You come in here and tell me there's been a double murder, one of them somebody I met and talked to only two days ago. You get me curious as hell—by sitting on my questions till you've finished yours—and then you're going to walk out on me? Nuts. You stay right there."

Conn strode out into the kitchen and a minute later came back with two fresh cans of beer. He handed Charlie Barrett one. "Now give," he said.

Charlie laughed. "Darry, I plumb forgot you're a what-you-may-call-it—a connoisseur of crime. All right, I can't spare a *lot* of time, but then again we don't know much yet so I guess I can brief you. And one more beer won't kill me.

"Okay, this morning at seven-fifty a call came in. Body found in an alley back of Wilshire. Not right *in* the alley, parking area just off it.

"At first it looked like an ordinary slugging and robbery. Wallet gone, no identification. Death from a blow on the back of the head with something hard and heavy—could have been a pistol or a wrench. We brought the body in—"

"Thought you said it was a double murder," Conn interrupted.

"It was. Keep your pants on; I'll get to that part of it. We brought him in and got some good pix for identification and a couple of the boys went out and started canvassing stores in the neighborhood to see if anybody knew him. No dice on that. Meanwhile an autopsy showed the cause of death to be just what we already knew it was and put the time of death somewhere around midnight, give or take an hour or two.

"So—outside of, of course, we checked with L.A. to see if they had any missing redheads—that was the way it stood when I came on at noon."

"Noon?"

"Yeah, I'm working a kind of swing shift this week. Start at noon. We switch around. Anyway, about half past twelve the cap calls me and Pete Kuzwa—you've met him, Darry; we're working as partners now—in and tells us there was just a call from a Mrs. Norbell who runs a rooming-boarding house on Worth Street and she was worried because a boarder of hers hadn't been home last night and hadn't showed for lunch. And he'd got a description from her and the guy was a redhead and the rest of the description fitted the stiff we'd found earlier. So would Kuzwa and I go around with one of the pix and get an identification and see what else we could pick up, if it was the right guy.

"So we did. So the Norbell dame busted out crying when we showed her the morgue pic; Atkins had roomed with her two years and she'd got fond of him. We got her quieted down and got the dope. She'd seen him last the evening before, 'round five-thirty.

"Atkins had come home from work then and cleaned up on account he was having a birthday dinner with his girl—he'd already told Mrs. Norbell about it a couple days before so she wouldn't expect him at the table that evening. It was the girl's birthday, not his, but she was celebrating it by cooking him a meal at her place.

"She said a little after Atkins left a funny-looking guy—

we got a good description of him—came around asking for him and made it so important that she told him where Atkins was—the girl's name, that is, and let him look up her address in the phone book.

"We—Kuz and I—looked up the address too and high-tailed over to talk to the girl. Place over a store on Pico. No answer when we knocked, so we started checking neighbors to see if any of them knew where she worked. Found the superintendent of the apartments and she knew, a restaurant in towards town. Phoned there and found the girl had been due to work an early shift and hadn't showed up. So we got a key from the super and went in her apartment. Found her. Killed same way as Atkins, probably by the same weapon, only the blow was on top of her head toward the front. Either she was struck from the front when she opened the door or else she knew the murderer and let him in, stood facing him while he swung but didn't have time to duck or yell."

Conn asked, "Which of them was killed first?"

"We're not sure. Doc thinks it was Atkins, but he hasn't performed full autopsies yet. That'll show, if they did have dinner together—not that there's any reason to believe they didn't—and if so, he can tell pretty close just how long after eating each of them died."

"Was Atkins using his car—the convertible?"

"Yeah. It turned up this afternoon, parked a few blocks from where we found his body. Our guess is the murderer drove it after Atkins did. The steering wheel and most other things a driver would touch were wiped clean."

"Find out who the guy was who asked for Atkins at the rooming house?"

"Not yet, but we're pretty sure he's the killer. We've placed him in the girl's neighborhood, early in the evening and again late. We got a pretty solid description from the landlady and since he'd looked up the girl's address and was presumably heading that way, we used that description to ask around the neighborhood. None of the other tenants in the building had seen him but there's a tavern a block away and we located the night shift bartender and hit pay dirt. He was in there twice, once early in the evening—probably right after he left the rooming house and once late; after midnight, the bartender thinks, but he can't give us any closer than that. And each time he had one drink only, and used the telephone."

Without asking this time Conn went out into the kitchen for two more beers. Charlie Barrett pretended to scowl. "Trying to get me drunk so you can pump me?" he asked. "All right, but this is positively the last one, Darry. I got to meet Kuz again and get back on the job right after I eat."

Conn asked, "How do you figure the case, thus far?"

"Well—we haven't got even a guess on motive so far. But outside of that it figures fairly easy enough. The guy who asked at the rooming house—let's call him John Doe—is the boy we're looking for. Not much doubt about that.

"From the rooming house John Doe goes right to the girl's neighborhood but instead of busting up there he phones from the nearest tavern and talks to Atkins at the girl's place. And either he made an appointment to go up and see Atkins there or he made an appointment to meet Atkins somewhere later. More likely to meet him later. It figures better that way, since Akins didn't get bumped till late in the evening.

"So he meets Atkins later and bumps him. Then goes back to Pico and phones the girl's number a second time, gives her some song and dance that will get her to open the door if he drops up. Goes up and kills her."

"But why? I mean, naturally he had some motive for killing Atkins but he couldn't even have known the girl since he had to get her name at the rooming house and look up the number and address in the directory there."

"Had to kill the girl because she knew who he was, on account of the first phone call when he made the appointment with Atkins. That means his business with Atkins must have been more or less on the up and up and he gave his right name and he'd figure Atkins would have told the girl who the phone call was from and what it was about and the girl's story would put him on the spot."

Charlie took another pull on his beer. He said, "We figure that whatever his business with Atkins was, it didn't start out to be murder at all. Two reasons for that. See them?"

"I see one of them," Conn said. "If he'd been planning to kill Atkins he wouldn't have needed to ring the girl in at all by phoning Atkins there. He could just have waited outside till Atkins left, followed him and caught up with him somewhere. If he'd known when he made the phone call that he was going to kill Atkins he'd realize that, on account of the phone call, he'd have to do two murders instead of one and double his risk. But what's the other reason, Charlie?"

"Just as simple as that one. If he'd been planning murder he wouldn't have had to show himself at the rooming house and let the landlady get ready to give us a good description. He'd have phoned the rooming house instead; he'd at least have tried to set up a date with Atkins somewhere else. Then we wouldn't have a goddam thing on him. As it is, we'll get him. We'll find someone who knows Atkins who knows someone who fits that description. That's all it will take."

He sighed. "Unless, of course, we get something that changes the picture."

"Such as what?" Conn prompted.

"Such as finding out Atkins was mixed up in a racket, something like that. But it doesn't seem likely. Seems to have been living inside his income. Or just outside of it, since we can't find he had any saved, but he hasn't been living high or throwing any more money around than a mechanic's wages would account for."

"But you don't know how much he would have had last night?"

"Couldn't have been more than a hundred even with the ninety he got from you. That was in cash?"

Conn nodded.

"Even so, not enough to get himself murdered for. He was to have got paid today, Saturday. Wasn't to have worked; it was his day off. But he always dropped in for his money. And since he was always borrowing just before payday, they tell us at the shop, he wouldn't have had much more than he got from you, if he had all of that left. No, we figure his wallet was taken just as a blind and maybe to slow down identification. Not that the killer would have thrown away ninety bucks more or less."

Conn said, "But it's not enough to have led to murder. Especially if the killer figured that killing Atkins would make it necessary to go commit a second murder just to cover up the first. Did he rob the girl's place?"

"It had been searched, and the money was gone from her

purse. But he couldn't have got much there. Probably not as much as off Atkins."

"How do you figure that?"

"Girl had a savings account; we found the passbook in her purse. Two hundred and forty-some bucks. But the point is the book showed she'd been saving regular every week. Ten, twelve, sometimes as high as fifteen bucks. People who save that way, in regular savings accounts, don't also hide money under mattresses. People fit a pattern in the way they save, if they do save. If Rose Harper turns out to have more savings than that, it'll be war bonds or postal savings certificates or something in a box at her bank. We'll check with them next week."

He put down the beer can empty and stood. "Well, Darry, I got to run. But say, did I ask you this? You don't know anybody at all who also knew Atkins? No mutual friends, acquaintances, you never saw him with anybody else?"

"Nope. Positive. I just saw him the one time I told you about and he was alone then. Neither of us happened to mention any other people at all. And even our meeting and getting to talk to one another was pure accident, like I told you."

"Okay. Well—just the same you could know this guy, without knowing he had any connection with Atkins. Here's what John Doe looks like: Six feet tall, about one-eighty pounds, smooth shaven, roundish face with a kind of wide jaw. No glasses. The dame thinks his eyes and hair are both dark but isn't sure about the hair; he didn't take his hat off. Wore a dark blue suit, white shirt and tie; wears—or wore—a dark felt hat with the brim turned down all around."

Conn shook his head. "Afraid it doesn't mean a thing to me, Charlie. But I wish you luck. Atkins seemed like a nice kid."

Her name was Joyce Williams, Joyce said, quite surprised that she should have been asked. Did whoever answered the phone where Claude Atkins roomed always ask who was calling please instead of just calling the person you asked for to the phone? Businessmen's secretaries protected their bosses that way, but she'd never heard of a rooming house landlady demanding to know who was calling when you asked for one of her roomers. It had almost caught Joyce off base into saying she was Joyce Dugan but she had remembered that Claude didn't know yet that she'd been married and so the name Dugan wouldn't mean anything to him.

And now, after asking who was calling, the woman was saying, "Mr. Atkins is not here. May I have your number for him to call you back?"

"No, thank you," Joyce said, and hung up.

She stood there a moment in the booth, staring at the telephone and wondering whether to be hurt or mad. She was a little of both, she decided.

He'd said so definitely that he'd be there, would make a point of being there, if she'd call at noon, and he hadn't been. Or if he had been there at exactly noon (it was ten minutes past now) but hadn't waited, hadn't given her even ten minutes' grace, that was even worse.

Had he completely forgotten their date, forgotten that she was going to call? If he hadn't, he could at least have left a message for her. She realized now that *could* have been why the landlady had asked who was calling; Claude could have told her "If I'm not back by noon and a girl named Joyce Williams calls, will you tell her—" But he hadn't left a message or the landlady would have given it to her.

She went out of the phone booth (it was in a restaurant where she had just eaten an early lunch) and out of the restaurant, stood a moment on the sidewalk outside wondering what to do.

Should she go back to her new room and go back to the job of straightening things up and putting things away and getting settled down? That was what she had intended to do after calling Claude and until whatever time he said he would come around to pick her up.

But she didn't feel like doing it now. Now that the Sunday afternoon she'd looked forward to was spoiled. And it *was* spoiled; she wasn't going to make a little fool and an eager beaver of herself by calling back again, and there wasn't any way Claude could get in touch with her.

Not until tomorrow, anyway. He knew where she

worked and he could drop in. Or if he was working he could phone. And if he had a good explanation or if he was contrite enough even if he had a weak one, then she'd forgive him and they could make another date instead. But after his saying he'd be there for her call and then not being there or even leaving a message, it was certainly up to him to make the next move. It was certainly not up to her.

But it spoiled everything for today. She'd been so cheerful and happy until now. Because of her date with Claude, the first date in a long, long time that she'd really looked forward to. Because of her good luck in finding, after a day's hard hunting yesterday, a room that was *so much* nicer than the one she'd given up at Mrs. Prescott's, and that cost her no more. It was fully half again as big and seemed even more so because it had a studio couch instead of a bed. And the couch was comfortable to sleep on. And it would be a good room for summer because there was cross-ventilation, windows on two sides, one of the windows opening right onto a fire escape. On the fourth floor and at the back of the building, it was far enough from the street that she wouldn't be bothered by traffic noises. A wonderful room. She was glad now that she'd had that spat with Mrs. Prescott and had given notice.

But she didn't want to go back to it now that she wouldn't be waiting there for Claude to get her.

Should she treat herself to the consolation prize of a movie? Or should she phone one or several of her friends to give them her new address and to find out whether they had plans for the afternoon? She decided that she didn't really want to see anybody today (now that she wasn't going to be seeing Claude). The movie won. That is, if the movies would be open this early. She thought they would. Some of them, at least, ran continuously from noon on Sundays.

She started walking toward Third Street, a few blocks away.

There were two theaters there only a block apart and another just around the corner from Third on Santa Monica Boulevard.

The first one she came to, the Strand, was open and the two pictures looked as though they were all right. One of them was a musical, with good singing and dancing stars, and the other a crime or suspense movie; she'd never heard of it but the cast looked good so it couldn't be really a B picture.

She bought a ticket and went in, found herself a seat where she liked to sit, about halfway down. The crime picture was on and it must have been on for a little while because she couldn't get the hang of it. Anyway, she found herself thinking about Claude Atkins and wondering what had happened, whether he'd really actually forgotten what he'd told her about being home at noon or whether something really important had kept him from being there.

Maybe she should give him one more chance, call once more in case he'd been trying to get home by twelve to take her call but had been unavoidably delayed. It was a little after half past twelve now, and—

No. Maybe it was silly pride, but there it was. She just wouldn't call back a second time. She'd feel such a fool if he still wasn't there. And she'd left her name so he'd know she had called when she'd said she would and if it really meant anything to him he'd do something about it tomorrow.

Little by little she began to get interested in the picture. It was a little bit—but not too much—like *Sorry, Wrong Number*. It was about a woman whom somebody wanted to murder, but in *Sorry, Wrong Number* the woman had known somebody was going to kill her, after a while anyway, and kept trying to get help and couldn't. In this one, the picture switched back and forth between the woman and the murderer and the audience knew that she was in danger, but she didn't. She didn't have the slightest suspicion that she was in danger. And the danger kept getting nearer and nearer as the picture went on.

It was scary, and she was glad when the picture ended and the musical started. She was glad things like that didn't really happen, didn't happen to people like her, anyway.

The musical was very good. Nice songs, wonderful dancing, and a light carefree plot that didn't mean much but was amusing and occasionally really funny. It was the kind of a movie Joe Dugan would have gone overboard for; he'd been a fair amateur singer and dancer himself and always appreciated real talent in either field. He'd always taken her to movies at least twice a week and they'd never missed a musical one. Sometimes when they were flush he'd take her to a real live revue if one happened to be playing at a downtown theater.

It had been wonderful, that year of marriage with Joe. But she had to forget, she told herself. It had been seventeen months and she had to forget.

Outside the theater the bright sunlight startled her momentarily, as it always startles one to come out of a darkened theater into broad daylight.

Only twenty past three. The trouble with going to a movie, even a double feature, so early; it doesn't kill all of the afternoon.

She sighed. Might as well go back to her room now and stay there, finish up the work she still had to do in getting settled. She could stop at a delicatessen and pick up something to fix for herself for dinner and for breakfast tomorrow morning. The room had a nice kitchenette. But she'd had this morning's breakfast and today's lunch out because she wanted to clean the kitchenette and wash all the dishes and cooking utensils before she used them and she hadn't got around to doing that yet. She'd do it next.

She found a delicatessen open and did her shopping, then walked on home. Up the three flights of stairs, back along the hallway toward the door of her room. She paused by the coin telephone in the middle of the hall and looked at the pad of paper on the little table under and beside it. If there had been a call for her while she was out there would be a message on that pad of paper. But how could there have been a call for her? Nobody knew the number yet. The pad was blank. (She should phone Mrs. Prescott and give her the new telephone number so if anyone called her at the old one, they could get the new number. She *had* given Mrs. Prescott the new address, but had not thought to make a note of the telephone number and so hadn't been able to give it to her.)

She went on back to the room and let herself in, resolutely started to work as soon as she slid into an apron. First the refrigerator, so she could put the food away. Then she stacked the dishes on the sink, dusted out the cupboard. Started on the dishes. She was drying the last one when she heard the faint sound of a telephone ringing. She put down the dish and the dishtowel and hurried to the door, opened it and went out into the hallway.

But another girl, a tall redhaired one, was coming from the opposite direction and was nearer. She said to Joyce, "I'll get it, honey," and Joyce stopped. But she stood there until she heard the redhead say, "Yes, this is Marilyn," before she went back into her room.

She opened the bottom part of the cupboard and looked at the pots and pans, sighed, decided she'd done enough work for today and that she'd take care of them tomorrow evening, except for any she had to use before then. She wouldn't need anything but the coffeepot tonight or in the morning; since she'd had a good hot lunch she'd settled at the delicatessen for bread and cold cuts for her supper, and some sweet rolls for breakfast.

She was hanging up her apron when there was a light knock on the door.

It was the tall redhead. "Hi," she said. "I'm Marilyn Peters. Just wondered if Mrs. God told you all our rules about the telephone and everything."

"Won't you come in?" Joyce said. "I'm Joyce Dugan. And if Mrs. God is Mrs. Burke, she told me that anybody who answers the telephone calls anybody else on the floor or takes a message on that pad on the table."

"Right, but not quite all of it, Joyce." Marilyn made herself comfortable on the studio couch. "She tell you who's in which room so you know what door to knock on?"

Joyce shook her head.

"Gimme paper and pencil then. There are four rooms besides this one and Mrs. God's up front, and two of them are doubles. You can't memorize six names all at once so I'll write them for you, and the room numbers. 'Course some people who phone might know the room number to tell you, but others wouldn't." She grinned. "Especially as the rooms aren't numbered."

Joyce found a pencil and a tablet of writing paper, watched while Marilyn made a rough sketch of the hall and wrote a name or pair of names behind each door.

"You'll know us all after a week or so," Marilyn said, handing over the tablet. "But this may come in handy until then. Oh, and one other thing. A rule we made up for ourselves. No limit to how long you use the telephone at a time—talk an hour if you want to—unless somebody else wants to use it or is expecting an incoming call. And it works both ways. If one of us is holding a marathon and you want to make a call or are expecting someone to be phoning you around that time, just a give signal and the phone is yours. Fair enough?"

"Sounds fine," Joyce said. She liked Marilyn and hoped she'd like the other girls as well. If she did, this was going to be a fine place to live.

Marilyn, she learned, was a stenographer for an insurance company. Two of the other girls worked in the Kresge store on Third Street, one clerked in a department store, one was a waitress and one a bookkeeper. On the side, Marilyn confided, two of them were interested in amateur theatricals and all of them were interested in men.

Joyce laughed and found herself telling about her own job, then being drawn into telling more and more about herself, about her marriage to Joe and his being killed in the accident and how she'd felt ever since, until now.

Marilyn nodded understandingly. "Joyce honey, you're right it's time you started dating again. And you came to the right place to get a good start at it, if the other girls like you as much as I do. We all got men on the string—men are a dime a dozen—and don't try to take any of our men, but all our men have friends. In a few weeks you'll find yourself wishing for a free evening once in a while."

Joyce laughed, pretending more amusement than she felt. (*That for you, Claude Atkins, she thought.*)

"In fact," Marilyn said, looking at her wrist watch, "I've got a dinner date for tonight and he's due to pick me up in about an hour. Ought to be home now, getting ready. Want me to call him and see if he's got a friend on the loose?"

"Oh, no, not tonight, please," Joyce said. Not this suddenly a blind date. She wanted time to get used to the idea. "I'm awfully tired," she explained. "All day yesterday hunting for a room, getting moved. Today getting settled down, unpacking, cleaning—you know. I should turn in early tonight."

"Okay, next time then. I'll talk to Tommy about you tonight and see who he might suggest for you, for a double on our next date." She stood up and stretched like a cat.

"Well, I'd better push along. Bathe and dress and put on war paint."

The room seemed brighter, less lonely, after Marilyn had gone. Brighter despite the fact that outside the sun was going down and the light was failing. Joyce sat there a few minutes in the bright dimness, enjoying the fact that she was thinking nothing, doing nothing, regretting nothing.

Feeling that she was on the threshold of living again, a new life. Maybe not a better one (nothing would ever be so wonderful as her year with Joe, nothing ever again) but at least something to look forward to.

She realized she was getting hungry and made herself coffee and a sandwich supper. Wondered whether she should call Mrs. Prescott and make sure there'd been no calls for her there, give Mrs. Prescott her new telephone number in case. Decided not to. There were only a very few people who might phone her there whom she'd even want to have her new number. It would be easier to phone those few people, either this evening or tomorrow evening. Rather than to listen to Mrs. Prescott's disapproving voice and have to ask a favor of her. If she did it that way, she'd never have to talk to Mrs. Prescott again, and that would be soon enough.

And face it, she told herself; your real reason for wanting to call there was the hope that Claude had somehow got that number and had been trying to reach you there. Claude *could* have got that number if he'd thought of calling Mr. Conn to ask how he could find her. But now Claude could just wait until tomorrow to explain and apologize for standing her up. And if he didn't, that was all right too.

She found herself humming happily as she straightened up after eating, found herself with enough ambition to go ahead and wash the pots and pans she'd decided to let go until tomorrow evening. (How did she know what might be happening tomorrow evening?)

There was another knock on the door. Marilyn again, but this time Marilyn beautifully dressed and in full war paint. Carrying a Sunday paper, an *Examiner.* "Honey," she said, "I'm through with this, was just going to throw it away, and then I remembered I didn't see a Sunday paper in your room. Did you have one?"

Joyce took the paper. "No, I didn't have one this week. I usually get one, but I forgot today. Thanks a lot. Won't you come in?"

"Thanks, I better not. Tommy's due any minute and I still got a few things to do. Be seeing you."

She put the paper down on the studio couch and finished her pots and pans, hung up the apron again. Golly, she thought, if only the other girls were anywhere near as likable and considerate as Marilyn, this would be a wonderful place.

It wasn't quite eight o'clock yet but she knew she wouldn't be going out again so she might as well take a shower and get into her pajamas before relaxing with the paper.

She made the shower a leisurely one and then, in flannel pajamas and a robe, she fixed herself a reading setup on the studio couch, moving a lamp to where it would give her good light and propping up pillows, making herself completely comfortable.

The funnies first. *Blondie and Dagwood, Bringing Up Father,* the *Katzenjammers, Donald Duck* and *Buzz Sawyer.*

The "Pictorial Review" section next, with its jokes and columns. Durling (she always liked him), *Here's Howe* and Louella Parsons. Then the *American Weekly;* she read the story and two of the articles, looked at the pictures. Then, as she always read a Sunday paper, the theater news, reviews of and ads for the new movies. Fashion news and the ads of some of the big downtown stores; maybe this coming week end, next week end, she'd take a bus downtown and pick out a new dress for herself, she decided. She hadn't bought any new clothes for herself for quite a while.

Getting sleepy, she yawned and almost didn't pick up the section with the front page. Just look at the headlines, she thought, unless there was something that specially interested her.

POLICE LINK TWO MURDERS, read a banner head across three columns, and under it a two-column subheading:

MAN, GIRL SLAIN
BY SAME KILLER,
POLICE BELIEVE

Crime stories seldom interested her, and she almost skipped reading farther, would have skipped it if she hadn't happened to notice the Santa Monica dateline at the start of the story.

She read on, and then gasped. *Claude Atkins!*

Murdered Friday night—why that was only hours after she'd seen him, had written the check and then cashed it for him!

And so *that* was why—

She read the story fast, the continuation on page three, and then turned back to the first page and read it a second time, slowly. Why? Why on earth would anyone have killed Claude Atkins? For that ninety dollars? Well, it could have been that if he'd flashed it in a tavern; people robbed for less than that and maybe the blow hadn't really been meant to kill. But the girl, Claude's fiancée the paper said (but they must have been wrong about that; Claude would hardly have made a date with Joyce if he'd really been engaged), why would the killer have gone to the girl's place and killed her too?

It was puzzling, and from the story she could see that the police were puzzled too.

Did the police know that Claude Atkins had had that ninety dollars in crisp new ten dollar bills? There was no mention of it in the story, nor about his having traded cars with Mr. Conn.

But they *must* know that part of it. From the license plates on the car, from the certificate of ownership that Mr. Conn had signed over to Claude. Surely if they hadn't talked to Mr. Conn about it yet, they would.

But, she realized, if the police *had* talked to Mr. Conn he couldn't have told them about that ninety dollars in cash because he would still be thinking she had just given Claude a check as he had told her to; he wouldn't know she'd cashed the check for Claude out of that envelope of new bills in the safe. So if the police did have the story from Mr. Conn they'd have it all wrong.

She put her feet down off the studio couch and sat on the edge of it, wondering if she should call the police tonight, right now, and tell them what she knew. Was it that important?

Well, maybe not important enough to call them tonight,

since it was almost ten o'clock now and she was in pajamas. And she certainly didn't want policemen coming up here to question her about details, especially on her second night in the room. (That would make a fine impression!) But if she called them tonight they'd either want to come here or ask her to come down to the station to tell her story (way over there on Main Street) and she'd have to dress and go out and heaven knows when she'd get to bed.

Oh, and that explained why Claude's landlady had asked her name when she'd called and had tried to get her to leave a phone number too. The police must have told her to handle any incoming calls for Claude that way, not to give any information but to try to find out who called him and get all the information she could.

And now the police would be looking for her to find out why she'd called Claude! But of course she'd given her maiden name; would they find her from that? Well, maybe they would eventually; if they checked Claude's life back far enough they'd find out he'd had dates in high school with a Joyce Williams, and they'd start checking from her records and address in high school, find out she'd married and what her married name was—yes, they could find her from that if they tried hard enough.

But when she told her story to them tomorrow she'd save them having to do that. She wondered if Mr. Conn's friend Sergeant Barrett was working on the case; the newspaper had mentioned or quoted only the Chief of Police. She hoped that Mr. Barrett was working on it; it would be easier to explain things to him than to a stranger.

She felt more excited than she'd felt in a long, long time. Here was a *murder* case, and she was in it. She was horrified, of course, at the thought that Claude had been killed, but after all she hadn't been in love with him or anything—not since the puppy love of high school—and she hadn't even seen him for six years until Friday afternoon. And if the police really had it right that he was engaged to another girl (What was her name? Oh yes, Rose Harper) then a date with him couldn't have led to anything serious anyway. And he'd been two-timing the other girl to have suggested one.

But however that might be it helped her pride a little to

know that he hadn't forgotten the date or stood her up.

Absurdly, she found herself crying.

Wondering, too, although she knew it was silly, whether she was bad luck to men; Joe getting killed in the accident, now Claude being murdered in an alley.

Resolutely she made herself ready the studio couch for sleeping, hung up the bathrobe and turned off the light, lay down to try to sleep. Only to try, for a long, long time. At one o'clock she was still wide awake and she knew that as far as sleeping was concerned she might just as well have got dressed and gone around to the police station to tell them her story.

But in one way she was glad that she hadn't. She really should talk to Mr. Conn first, explain things to him first, about why she'd thought he wouldn't mind if she cashed the check for Claude and tell him she hoped he didn't mind that she'd used part of that money in the envelope.

And then, if the police hadn't questioned Mr. Conn yet, quite probably he'd drive her over to the station and they could tell their stories together.

Or maybe, if his friend the detective sergeant was working on the case he'd just phone and have Barrett come around to the shop.

Another exciting thought struck her. Just maybe her story and Mr. Conn's together would enable the police to find the murderer! Because those ten dollar bills had been brand-new, fresh from the mint and obviously never used at all, just maybe all twenty of them (if it had been twenty) had consecutive serial numbers. And if they did have them from the ones that were still in the envelope they could tell what the numbers had been on the nine bills she'd given Claude. And the murderer must have those bills because the story said that Claude's wallet had been taken and she'd seen him put the bills in his wallet. All the police would have to do was to wait for those serial numbers to turn up and they'd have the murderer by tracing them back.

And then again she found herself crying quietly. (For Claude, or for Joe, or for both of them?)

She hoped Mr. Conn would be down early in the morning so they wouldn't lose any time going to the police.

Almost, for a moment, she decided it was important enough for her to phone Mr. Conn tonight. She wished she'd thought of it earlier, when she'd first read the story at ten o'clock. But it was too late now; he'd be sound asleep.

She wished that she could sleep. Finally she slept.

His name was Dean Bratten, Conn told the man behind the general delivery window at the Venice Post Office. And the letter he was expecting would have been mailed from Manhattan Beach, probably on Saturday. The clerk shuffled through the stack of letters in the B pigeonhole, handed over the second from the top and then kept on looking through the others. Conn waited until the clerk said, "Guess that's all."

Outside the post office he opened the envelope, dropped the bank deposit box key into his trousers pocket and put the slip from the storage company in his wallet. He crumpled the envelope and the piece of paper in which the key had been folded and put them in a trash container.

Two things again in his possession that tied him to murder. But the bank key would mean nothing once he'd taken the rest of the counterfeit money out of the safe deposit box. And after he'd added that money to the other things in the two suitcases in storage, and then had remailed the storage slip to himself, there'd be nothing to tie him to either counterfeiting or murder, nothing.

Nor anything left for him to do except the minor annoyance of having—say once a week until he was absolutely sure he was completely safe and completely unsuspected—to pick up the storage slip and remail it to himself.

Back to Santa Monica to the bank and then to Manhattan Beach and complete safety.

He drove cautiously, thinking how bad it would be if he had an accident now. Or even worse after he'd been to the bank and before he reached the storage company, with three thousand dollars in counterfeit on him when they went through his pockets at the hospital. In sealed envelopes, but they'd probably open them.

He found parking space only half a block from the bank, put two pennies in the parking meter for twenty-four minutes. Twelve minutes would be enough probably but what was an extra penny?

Walked to the bank. Had his hand on the knob when he saw the sign behind the glass of the door:

BANK CLOSED
LINCOLN'S BIRTHDAY
FEBRUARY 12TH

He swore. God damned bankers, *any* excuse to close a bank. The post office had been open (although he wished now that it hadn't), everything else was open. But banks— the God damned banks.

He walked back to his car, looked with a jaundiced eye at the silly parking meter with only one minute used out of twenty-four, then felt wry amusement at himself for being annoyed about a penny when his life was at stake.

Got in the car and sat behind the wheel.

No use swearing at banks or at Abraham Lincoln. This was nothing serious, just a postponement by twenty-four hours of the peace of mind he'd feel when, and not feel until, those three hundred bills in the deposit box were safe at the storage company with the other things that could incriminate him. All his eggs in one basket, but a safely hidden basket that the police would never find.

There was only one thing he had to decide now before he went to the shop. Was it worth while, for one day, to remail the key and the slip to himself so they wouldn't be in his possession between now and tomorrow morning when he could use them?

Of course it wasn't. God, he must be getting psychopathic to worry about such a little thing—two such little things—when there wasn't even a shadow of suspicion against him.

Charlie had been completely satisfied with his story. Had not even asked him what he'd been doing at the time of the murders. Hadn't, to begin with, even considered the matter important enough to bring his partner with him.

Still, reasonable precautions wouldn't hurt. He put the key back on his key ring with the others; it didn't show that it was a deposit box key and if asked he could say he'd forgotten what it was the key to. There were enough keys on the ring to make that reasonable; as a matter of fact there really were two small keys he couldn't place offhand. Besides, if they started checking with that kind of thoroughness they'd find out from his bank that he had a box there whether or not the key was on him.

The slip—well he could best hide it back at the shop. It could lie flat on the bottom of a galley of type in one of the racks and wouldn't be found by any search that didn't take the whole shop apart piece by piece and pi all the type in the place. Or, even better, it could lie between two sheets of paper in a stack of paper, in a shop stocked with paper of all kinds and sizes. Safe as houses.

He drove the four blocks to the shop and left the car in the usual place, the parking place just off the alley behind the back door. Let himself in with his key.

Joyce was already there. She'd opened the shop from the front at nine as she always did if he wasn't down ahead of her. She looked up from opening the day's mail. She looked excited about something.

"Oh, Mr. Conn," she said, "did you read about Claude Atkins? Being murdered, I mean?"

"Why, sure, Joyce; it was in all the Sunday papers."

"Oh. Did you go to the police about it? Tell them about the car and everything?"

"Yes. Rather, they came to me before I even knew about it from the papers. From the car registration slip, of course. I told them all about it. Not that the car trade had anything to do with what happened. Just routine checking."

"Well, Mr. Conn, I think I'd better go to them right away because I can tell them more."

A cold knot was forming in his stomach. "I don't think it's necessary, Joyce. I told them everything that would be of interest to them about it."

"But there are things you couldn't have known about it and that I do know. You see you told me just to give him a check and they're probably trying to find out where and when he cashed it, or rather if he did or not so they'd know how much money he had and—"

"I know you cashed it for him, because I came down to the shop Saturday to get some money for myself and I found the check in that envelope and ninety dollars gone, so I knew you'd cashed it for him."

"Oh." She sounded disappointed. "Was it all right for me to have used that money to cash it for him? He said you'd told him you'd pay in cash and—well, I tried to call you back on the phone but the line was busy and I thought it would be all right."

"Of course it was all right. But how did you happen to know the money was there? Not that it matters."

Careful, careful, he told himself. Be natural. Be interested, but play it down, don't make it seem important.

He still had his hat and coat on. He took them off and hung them up.

"—just by accident," Joyce was saying. "I know it was with your personal papers and I never take anything out of that part of the safe, but a sheaf of stuff *fell* out, just the day before. And that envelope fell with the flap open and I just couldn't help seeing it had ten dollar bills in it, brand-new ones."

"Oh. I just wondered how you happened to know about it. But it's perfectly all right. About the police, I mean. Since I already knew about it by the time the police looked me up, they know he had the money in cash."

"Did you tell them it was all in brand-new bills?"

Danger danger. If he said yes when he hadn't and then Joyce went to the police despite him, he'd be caught in a lie and that would be just the start of it. Once there was even a *touch* of suspicion—brand-new bills—from an engraver—Charlie's having kidded him back when about how easy an engraver ought to be able to make money—his omissions in his story to Charlie, letting Charlie think (without saying so, of course) that he himself had paid that ninety dollars in cash at the time of the sale and leaving Joyce out of it—Charlie's too-close-for-comfort analysis of the reason why Rose had had to be killed after Claude—Charlie's needing only a motive to put him on the right track, and if he *got* on that track, especially today before Conn could get that counterfeit out of the bank—God.

But if he said no to Joyce, that he hadn't told the police the ninety was in new tens then she'd really know she had good reason to go to them and he wouldn't be able to stop her. He was trapped and had to lie.

"Of course," he told Joyce.

"Oh," she said, sounding a little disappointed again.

"But listen, Mr. Conn, did you think of this? Those were all *brand-new* bills and they hadn't been in circulation; you could tell that just by looking at them. Did you get them all from the bank at the same time? If you did, and if the *bank* had just got them, from the mint or from wherever banks get new money from, then all the serial numbers would run in a row. And if they do, why then, you'll know the serial numbers—or at least serial numbers *close* to the ones I gave Claude out of that envelope. And since the man who killed Claude *did* take his money, even if that wasn't the real reason—the papers didn't think so; I guess because that girl was killed too—why he's going to spend some of those bills and then the police will get him."

She turned and looked toward the safe, still unopened. "You didn't take *all* of the other bills from that envelope, did you, Mr. Conn? Or spend them all?"

The cold knot back, tightening.

Think, be calm, think.

He smiled at her. "Of course I didn't spend it all, Joyce. But the numbers weren't consecutive. I know that because they didn't all come from the same place. In fact, no two of them from the same place at the same time. It was a little— well, call it a little vacation fund of mine that I was saving up. Over quite a few months. And every time I'd happen to get a brand-new ten dollar bill I'd add it to the fund—but I never added two at a time; just couldn't afford it, even if I had got two new ones or more in the same haul from cashing the same check or whatever. Too bad it was that way; if the numbers had really been in order then you had a swell idea."

Don't breathe yet; this isn't over yet. But you're still on top. Still nothing you haven't covered, nothing that the police should be told by Joyce, damn her.

She was smiling too. "Gee, and I thought I had such a wonderful idea. Here I thought I was going to help the police—and I didn't know you knew about my cashing the check for him and I hoped those serial numbers—and everything—"

He laughed a little. Quite naturally, he thought. He wanted a cigarette but he didn't dare try one then because he was afraid his hands would shake.

He said, "Sorry, Miss Hildegarde Withers, but I'm afraid

you're out of luck on helping the police on this one."

But I've got to fire her. Sooner or later Charlie will drop in and he and she seem to like one another, always swap a few remarks and—

And Jesus, what if Charlie should drop in today? He hadn't been in the shop for almost a month, but what if some slight angle on this deal should bring him in? *Today!* Tomorrow, any time before he could get rid of Joyce, would be bad enough but after tomorrow at least the money would be out of the deposit box; tomorrow, after as long as it took him to get into the box after the bank opened and thence to Manhattan Beach, Charlie would have to scratch for proof, whatever he suspected—

Unless, even then, the landlady at Atkins' rooming house might say, when confronted, that Conn "reminded her" of Charlie's John Doe, as Atkins had noted a similarity between Conn and Conn in that disguise— Or the bartender on Pico—

Danger. Christ, how had he thought himself safe?

Joyce sighed. Ruefully, "And here I thought I *had* something. I didn't get around to reading a paper until late yesterday evening, too late to go around then and—oh, well."

He patted her shoulder. "Don't let it get you down." He took out a cigarette and lighted it and his hands were steady. "Anything special in the mail? Or did you finish opening it?"

"It's all open, but I just skimmed it. Two you'll probably want me to answer. Want to tell me what to tell them now? This one's from the credit manager at Lafayette Paper and I guess you know—"

"I guess I know. I'll dictate later, Joyce. You catch up on posting to the ledger. I got to get type set on that announcement from the Bayerly Stores."

He stood up and flicked ash from his cigarette at the ash tray. And hit it.

Walked back to the Linotype and turned the switch that would start melting the type metal in the pot. Went to his own desk and started looking for and then looking over the copy for the Bayerly job.

Thinking. What are the odds on Charlie dropping in today, this week? How soon can I fire Joyce? What can I tell her as a reason? How little notice can I give?

It's got to be good. It's got to be good.

Improvise. The Perfect Criminal can always—

Pretend to get sick, seriously sick, today, starting now? Tell Joyce you know what this is and it's something that's been coming on for a while, that you'll have to close down the shop a while, maybe indefinitely, and you can't expect her to wait, that you'll pay her a couple of weeks in advance and that she'd better—?

But then you'll *have* to close down the shop. And eat what and use what to pay bills? And if Joyce, with all the time on her hands that giving her salary in advance for nothing would give her, should decide to go talk to the police anyway, then there's *another* lie and an obvious one; what's wrong with you and what doctor told you so? Too dangerous.

That silly rhyme his father had told him more than once; how did it go? *What a tangled web we weave, when first we practice to deceive?* Something like that.

But his father had died when he was eighteen and his mother when he was twenty. And what did Joyce know of that or of the fact that he had been an only child? If, today, he pretended he had a telegram from a younger sister who was arriving tonight, looking for a job, and— Ridiculous. Even more easily disproven, if Joyce went to the police anyway.

A hand touched his shoulder lightly, and he jumped. Turned. It was Joyce.

"Uh—Mr. Conn."

"Yes, Joyce?"

"Before you get working on the Linotype. Would it be all right if I take a little longer on my lunch time today—maybe a half an hour over; I don't think it ought to take longer than that—if I work later tonight to make up for it?"

"Why, sure, Joyce. But why?" The twisting knot in his guts again. Had he lost this soon?

"To go to the police station. I've got to talk to them."

"But they know everything you could tell them. I told you—"

"Not that, Mr. Conn. Something else. There's something else they've got to know. We got off talking about my cashing the check and the new money and all that, but that's not all. You see, I *knew* Claude. We were in high school together. We hadn't seen each other for six years, about, before he came in Friday afternoon, but he made a date with me and I was supposed to take a ride with him Sunday afternoon and I phoned him after he was dead and—I've got to tell them because they're looking for me under the wrong name."

Oh God, he thought, oh Jesus God. But what was the girl talking about?

He repeated it blankly. "The wrong name?"

"Uh-huh. You see—I guess I told you this when I first started here eight or nine months ago, but maybe you forgot—Dugan is my married name, Mr. Conn. My husband died a year and a half ago. We'd been married only a year and I'd known him only a few months before that. And when Claude and I went together in high school was six years ago, so the name Dugan wouldn't have meant anything to him and I didn't think to tell him about that Friday. See?"

He didn't see. He just looked at her.

"And he made a date to pick me up for a ride Sunday afternoon but I was moving Saturday afternoon and I didn't yet know where I was going to be moving to, so I had to call *him*, Sunday noon."

"But—" Still a blank.

"Don't you see, Mr. Conn? I had to call him and his land-lady answered—he was already dead then and the police must have told her to get the name and phone number of anyone who called him and not to give *out* any information. So she asked me my name and I remembered Joyce Dugan wouldn't mean anything to Claude because he didn't know I'd been married so I gave her my maiden name, Joyce Williams, and I didn't leave a phone number because I was calling from a pay station just then and besides—well, I just didn't want to leave a number for him to call because I was calling at the time he said he'd be waiting for my call and I thought he was standing me up."

It was too complicated; for the moment it didn't register. He said, "I don't get it, Joyce. Why does that mean you should go to the police?"

"Because, don't you see, they're wasting time looking for a Joyce Williams who phoned him Sunday. They'll find me all right—I mean, if they check back far enough they'll find he went to high school with a Joyce Williams and had dates with her. And since I've stayed right here in Santa Monica all the time it won't be hard for them to find out when I married and my married name and—but look at all the work I'll save them if I just go around and explain that I was the Joyce Williams who phoned him!"

And, of course, tell them all the rest of it while you're at it. They'll want to know the whole story, where and when the date was made, and out will come nine brand-new bills and the omissions and evasions in my story to Charlie and—

Jesus.

He sighed. He said, "Of course if that's the case, Joyce, you'll have to explain to them. As you say, they'll get to you anyway—" He managed a chuckle or what he thought was one. "—and if they do it that way they might even start suspecting you. So okay, take as long as you need for lunch."

"Thanks, Mr. Conn." She went back to her desk.

Nine thirty-seven. Joyce went to lunch at half past twelve. (Conn at eleven-thirty; he liked an early lunch and it let him avoid crowded restaurants or lunch counters.) A little less than three hours. Less than three hours to forestall—or at least to *stall*—the inevitable.

Fingers moving automatically over the Linotype keys. Eyes reading copy on the clipboard and sending messages to the fingers which keys to touch. Click of mats down the channels and over the star wheel. Send a line to cast; start the instant the elevator drops. All automatic. *Think.*

Joyce will go to the police. Can't stop her.

They'll guess. They'll see the motive. Told Charlie no lies but Joyce's story will point up the omissions and make them even more significant than if told originally. Brand-new bills out of an envelope apart, in private papers.

The motive; all the police would need.

This is it. End of the trail. Unless—

He thought, *but I don't want to kill Joyce; I like Joyce; and it would be useless anyway, tying another motive to the shop, to myself, would bring suspicion—*

Wait. Would it?

If Joyce was dead, no one would ever know about that check, would ever be able to disprove his story that he'd paid Atkins cash the evening of the trade; no one would know that Atkins had called at the shop to collect; no one would ever know about the envelope in the safe with the new bills.

The stub Joyce must have made for the check? It would be the last check written in the book and if he didn't have her write any more checks this morning then he could take out the staple, put in another stub with check attached, a virgin one, and there'd be no record that such a check had ever been written or that Atkins had ever been at the shop.

Or that he had known Joyce through the shop or through Conn.

Because, of course, he hadn't. They'd known one another a lot more years than he, Conn, had known either of them. And the police were already looking for a "Joyce Williams," who had phoned Atkins after he was dead, and when they found both Joyces were the same Joyce—what a beautiful red herring *that* would be. Why, they'd wonder, had Joyce used her maiden name on that call? Why had she—apparently—tried to hide her identity?

It would be a beautiful mess-up, a beautiful cover-up.

Pale February sunshine through a windowpane across his hands, idle on the keyboard. He stared at them.

And if Joyce's body was not found until—well, until tomorrow afternoon, then by that time the bank deposit vault would be clear of anything incriminating, the slip from the storage company would again be in the mail to a general delivery address—

Police looking for a psychopathic killer who for whatever mad reason had killed Atkins and two women connected with him—one of whom had made a mysterious phone call to him under her maiden name—

Oh, yes, in a *sense* he'd be in the middle. His one admitted contact with Atkins, his having employed Joyce for eight months or however long it had been (but they could prove no connection with the other girl; it would make no sense that he would have motive to kill the three of them).

The Perfect Criminal can always improvise. Such as—suppose he killed Joyce in her room tonight and meanwhile got back from the suitcases in storage the things he had taken from the shoebox in the Harper girl's closet, and suppose he left in Joyce's room the letters of Atkins to his fiancée—? There'd been three or four of them and he'd glanced at one; it had not been dated and it had started "Honey:" and not "Dear Rose:"—

That and Joyce's phone call to Atkins would add to a triangle—

By all means, the same weapon, the revolver used as a bludgeon, the same signature—

He was staring at Joyce. When had he turned around on the stool in front of the Linotype?

Her figure, especially her breasts so clearly outlined by the tightly fitting, closely woven sweater, so like Myrtle's. Her hair blonde like Myrtle's. But so much younger. If he had met Myrtle at that age—? Why Myrtle *had* been almost that young when he'd first met her four years ago. Twenty-seven, as against Joyce's—was it twenty-four? Or had Myrtle given herself the benefit of a few years in telling her age, despite the fact that he was older than she? Joyce *seemed* so much younger, almost a child compared—

He shook his head to clear it of a line of thought that meant nothing, led nowhere. The Perfect Criminal never—

Joyce looked around (because the Linotype wasn't running?) and caught his eye.

"Oh, Mr. Conn, I moved Saturday. To a new room. I've put my new address and phone number in the address book. It's on Colorado."

"Oh. Walking distance?"

"Yes, this time it is. And a lot nicer than the other room I had." She smiled. "Had a kind of tiff with my landlady at the old place and that's why I moved, but gee I'm glad I *had* that argument with her. This new place is so much better."

"By yourself? Or with another girl?"

"By myself. I'd hate it any other way. Guess I'm just not—not the type to like living with another girl."

She opened a drawer and he saw she was taking out the checkbook. He asked quickly, "Were you going to write a check, Joyce?"

"A couple of small ones. Remember Friday you told me to send checks for the bills from Asplund Paper Company and to the type metal company as soon as I got around to it? I didn't have time Friday on account of folding those hand-bills and—"

"Don't," he said sharply. "I mean, since you didn't get to it Friday wait another few days. No real hurry on them and

I want to keep the bank balance up till I collect on a few of my own accounts. Don't send out any checks today."

"Okay, sure. But they're both small checks and if I mark the one I wrote out for Claude *canceled*, since we cashed it for him ourselves, and we can just tear it up, or—oh, of course you won't tear it up because it's proof you paid it out and anyway the police may want to see it."

"I'll take care of that. But don't write any more checks, even small ones, till I tell you to, Joyce." He hesitated, seeking a logical reason. "You see I might have a chance in the next day or three to buy some equipment from another printer who's going out of business. But it would have to be cash on the line and even a few dollars difference in the account might keep me from picking up something I need."

"Okay. I see you *did* buy something new, since Friday. That little thing over in the corner. Just what is it?"

"A hand press, Joyce. No, I didn't buy it. Had it at home, since you've been here. Just happened to bring it down Saturday in case I'd want it here."

"Oh. You were doing some printing at your house?"

She wasn't looking and he closed his eyes. Joyce or me, he thought; it's got to be one of us now. One more little thing she'll tell, one more little thing that will be drawn out of her when the police start the questioning—

He said lightly, "Sure. Been printing myself some money."

Joyce giggled appreciatively. "Ten dollar bills? Was that what was in the separate envelope?"

Now? he wondered. *Is she that close? Or is she kidding? She's kidding; that giggle was real. But when the police start drawing her out, she'll remember that. And—*

"Yep," he said. "Didn't they look like genuine ones?"

He swiveled back to the Linotype, started the mats clicking again quickly, before she could answer. He wanted to end *that* line of conversation quickly, before— Well, she wasn't stupid. And she knew more than the police knew already, a hell of a lot more.

Set: *Long wearing 100% virgin wool, worsted and flannel, firm finished, alive with colorful 'splash' yarns. Highly wrinkle-resistant. Full draping with one-button single breasted coat, dressy peaked lapels. Trousers have continuous waistband, zipper. All men's sizes. Blue, tan, and gray. ONLY*

Filled the stick and took it to the bank to dump the type, brought it back, started another.

What if Charlie Barrett should drop in now? No, he wouldn't, not before noon. He starts work at noon, probably isn't even up yet. Besides, working on this case, he has the excuse (think of some question he'd think unimportant) to drop in on city time instead of his own time.

Joyce can't be here this afternoon. Charlie not around for almost a month but right now too much chance of his realizing he can combine business and pleasure and drop in, alone or with Kuzwa, on city time. Have to get Joyce away on some pretext, keep her away from noon on. Can't kill her today, not until late tonight in her room. Can't have her body found until late enough tomorrow to have taken care of the bank and the storage company. Or to hell with the storage company, save an hour and a half not to have to drive to Manhattan Beach and back. Gun can't be traced to me so leave it in Joyce's room. Package money and storage slip, mail to myself general delivery. Can be here, shop open, ready even if Joyce's body found by nine-thirty. If they do suspect me, there'll be no shred of evidence, can't hold me. But have to be sure not followed whenever pick up general delivery and make trip to warehouse.

It would work. Sure, it would work.

Easy, if Joyce's new room—

SHEET BLANKETS. *Assorted cotton plaid, deep napped. Pink, blue, green. Regularly $1.49. ONLY*

He carried the full stlck to the bank and dumped the type on the stone, went back to the machine and replaced the stick. But instead of sitting down he lighted a cigarette and strolled over to where Joyce was working, around in front of her desk and leaned back against the counter behind him.

She looked up. "Yes, Mr. Conn?"

"Joyce," he said. "Your taking a new room reminds me. I've been thinking about selling the house I'm living in— silly for a widower to keep a house all to himself even if it's only a small one. What I'd get out of my equity in it wouldn't be much, but it would give me a little more capital to put in the business. And just taking a room somewhere myself. Probably cost me a lot less than taxes and upkeep on the house, not to mention interest on the mortgage."

He gestured vaguely. "But it's been so many years since I have roomed anywhere that I don't know what the score is. Since you just moved and must have been looking around first you can probably tell me. Are rooms scarce now? In Santa Monica, I mean; I'd want to live fairly close to the shop here."

"Why, no. It's not hard to find a room. I was lucky to find a *nice* one, one I really like, in just one day's hunting, Saturday. But if you took your time looking around, you wouldn't have any trouble. Especially because you probably wouldn't mind paying more than I'm paying."

He smiled deprecatingly. "I doubt that, Joyce. I wouldn't want anything fancy. Listen, it's none of my business what you're paying so don't tell me if you don't want to, but if you don't mind it would give me sort of an idea—"

"I don't mind. Ten dollars a week at the new place and as it happens that's exactly what I was paying at the other one, but that's for a housekeeping room."

Conn said, "I guess I'd want a housekeeping room—not that I cook meals for myself often but I always get my own breakfast, hate to have to go out for it. Well, ten dollars sounds cheap enough. Does your landlady clean the room every day or do you have to do that yourself?"

"Oh, I have to do that myself. With maid service a room like that runs a little more."

"Well, even if it ran twice that I'd be saving money, I think, over what it costs me now. Do you have a private entrance, or do you have to go through somebody's living room or anything like that?"

"A private entrance, I guess you'd call it. Probably that floor—it's the fourth floor, the top one—was laid out for one big flat originally but it was remodeled into separate rooms. Mrs. Burke—" Joyce giggled a little. "—the other girls call her Mrs. God but I haven't found out why yet—lives in the front room and rents out the others; they all open off the hallway so they all have private entrances. She just rents to girls, though."

Conn smiled. "I wasn't thinking of trying to outbid you for it. I'm just trying to get a general idea, Joyce. You said it's on Colorado? Traffic noises bother you?"

"Oh, no. I can't even hear them. My room's way at the back of the building. Come to think of it, I've got two private entrances. My back window opens right on the fire escape, over the alley."

"Aren't you afraid of burglars?"

Joyce laughed. "What would they steal? Anyway, I was only kidding about it being a private entrance. You know how fire escapes are. You can go down them but not up; they start at the second floor."

But, Conn thought, in an alley, in the dead of night, you could go up one if you parked a car under it, climbed on top of the car and pulled yourself the rest of the way.

Did she lock the window off the fire escape? He fumbled for a question that might, without making her suspicious, get her to tell him. Then quickly dropped the idea as he realized that if she were led into thinking about it she might lock it tonight even though she wouldn't otherwise.

If she did lock it—well, the fire escape would still let him locate her room from the outside and then, upstairs in the hallway, judge which door led to it. (He couldn't very well whisper, "It's me, Claude, honey—" But he'd think of something.)

He said, "Thanks a lot, Joyce. I got a lot better idea now what a room will run me if I do decide to sell the house."

The cigarette was short now and he turned around to stub it out in an ash tray on the counter. Over his shoulder he said, "Hope I'm as lucky as you are in getting a room way back from the street, quiet. I'm a light sleeper; least little noise always wakes me up."

"I'm just the other way around," Joyce said. "Once I get to sleep I really pound my ear. I could sleep through a bomb going off." She smiled. "I did, once.

"Well, not really a bomb, but an explosion. A gas main explosion right outside where I was rooming then. It shook the house, they told me afterward, and everybody else woke up and was scared stiff but I slept right through it."

"You're lucky," Conn said.

"But it's funny, I don't need an alarm clock. You'd think a sound sleeper would, but all I have to do is decide I want to get up at seven o'clock or whatever, and I wake up almost to the minute. About that check I made for Claude and he endorsed, Mr. Conn. You want me to deposit the check? Or shall I get it out of the safe and just put it with canceled checks so you got a record of paying it?—I guess his endorsement shows he got the money whether you deposit it or not—and then I can just mark the check stub 'Void' and add ninety dollars to the balance."

"No, don't do that," Conn told her. "Let the stub alone and we'll just deposit the check. But not today because it isn't here."

She looked a question at him but didn't ask it.

He explained. "I told you I came in Saturday to get some money. I just took that envelope out of the safe without looking in it until after I got home. And I didn't think to bring the check down this morning. I'll bring it down tomorrow."

"Okay. I don't think the bank will be open today anyway. It's Lincoln's Birthday."

"That's right, it is," Conn said. "I'd forgotten. Well, I'm not getting any work done this way. Back to the salt mines."

Back to the Linotype.

WOOL SKIRTS. *Group of all-wool skirts, flannels, tweeds, checks, plaids, solids, sizes 10 to 18. Reg. 5.99 to 7.99. NOW*

Now it would be easy. Oh, there was a risk, of course, but a calculated risk and only a slight one. Just as there'd been a calculated risk on the last two murders. The risk, for instance, that the blow through the doorway at the Harper girl could have missed and let her scream.

Much less risk than that tonight. The only one he could foresee was the risk of being seen going up the fire escape and, if he waited until between two and three in the morning (when she'd be sleeping most soundly anyway) that risk would be a slight one. With what he knew now, he wouldn't have to take the risk of the hallway and knocking on her door. He had at home a short crowbar that should make an excellent jimmy to open the window if she did lock it.

Yes, he could consider tonight already planned.

Now he could concentrate on the more immediate problem, how to keep her away from the police until then. And how to get her out of the shop this afternoon so she wouldn't be here if Charlie—or any other detective—should drop in.

Gradually a plan took shape in his mind. Not too complicated. But not so simple as to be obvious.

First step, take his own lunch hour half an hour early so he could get back here by twelve, get rid of her then.

Charlie Barrett wouldn't be here *at* twelve; that was when he reported in at the station. But if he made Conn's the first stop he could be here before half past twelve when Joyce usually went to lunch.

At eleven he stood up from the Linotype and stretched. Started back to wash the ink off his hands with Lava Soap, but stopped and turned toward Joyce.

"Taking off now, Joyce," he said. "Want to see a man about a job I might talk him into giving us. I'll go to lunch from there. Back at the usual time."

"All right. I got only five or ten more minutes on this job. What do you want me to do next?"

"Ummm—might run me up a list of accounts payable and accounts receivable, as they stand right now. I'm thinking *damn* seriously about selling that house to get some more capital for the business and before I decide I want to see just how I stand."

"Okay. And if I get that done before you're back?"

"That ought to hold you," he said. Especially as he'd be back sooner than she expected, before noon. "If you do finish, do some proofreading on the stuff I set this morning. I ran off all the galleys except the last one on the proof press."

He went back and washed up, got his coat. Went to the door. "So long, Joyce."

"Oh, Mr. Conn." He stopped and turned.

"Is your friend Mr. Barrett working on the case?"

"Yes, he is. Why?"

"I was just thinking. I don't want to have to take *too* long on my lunch hour and they may want to ask an awful lot of questions. I was just thinking it might save time if I called up and kind of make an appointment. And if Mr. Barrett is working on the case I guess I'd rather talk to him than to a stranger."

He sighed. God, what if she'd thought of that a few minutes after he'd left?

He said mildly, "I guess it might be a good idea, Joyce. Can't hurt anyway. And yes, you might as well talk to Charlie and let him get the credit for treeing the mysterious Miss Williams who put in that call. Glad you thought of it." He partly turned to go, then turned back. "But don't phone before twelve—that's when he goes on duty."

"All right, Mr. Conn."

"In fact, wait till a quarter after. They have roll call and stuff like that and he wouldn't be leaving the station before half past twelve in any case. Be seeing you."

Outside, walking down the boulevard, he had to put his hands in his pockets because they were shaking so badly. What a narrow one *that* had been.

But how easily he'd been able to improvise a way around it.

But it was all right now. Except that he'd have to make sure to get back well before twelve. Not to take a chance on her jumping the gun a few minutes.

He wanted a drink to steady his nerves and stopped in a combination bar and restaurant so he could have both that and a sandwich without having to make two stops. He ate his sandwich at the bar and had to watch himself to avoid wolfing it down because of his worry and impatience to get back, despite the fact that he was going to have time to kill rather than the other way around.

He couldn't get back before ten minutes of twelve at the earliest and five of would be better. He'd have to pretend to have seen the potential customer and to have run into Charlie and talked to him as well.

And allowing ten minutes to get back (it had taken him seven to get to the bar) he still had fifteen minutes to kill when he'd finished the sandwich.

Decided one more drink would solve the problem and wouldn't hurt him. Ordered a highball this time and helped kill time by trying to ration it mathematically so he would be sipping it at a uniform rate and take the last sip at exactly a quarter to twelve.

At seventeen minutes to twelve he downed the remainder at a gulp, hurried out, and had to watch his pace on walking back to keep himself from running or almost running.

"Gee, you're back early, Mr. Conn," Joyce said. "Or didn't you eat yet?"

"Yeah, I ate. Ran into Charlie Barrett—of all people, since we were just talking about him—and had a sandwich with him on his way to work. And you won't have to phone him."

He hung up his coat.

"Oh, you mean you made an appointment for me to talk to him?"

"Yes, but not around at the police station. I told him in general what it was you had to tell him—not all the little details, I'll let him ask you about those—and asked if he wanted you to come around there. He said he sure wanted to talk to you but he'd much rather drop in on you early this evening if you were free then. He's got some important things to do right away after he reports in today. Are you free this evening, Joyce?"

"Why, yes. I mean, I hadn't planned anything." She sounded disappointed, had probably been looking forward to the adventure of a call at the police station—and a long lunch hour.

"Good. I didn't have your new address or telephone number with me to give to him, but he said he'd phone here some time this afternoon and get them. You said you put them both in the book, didn't you?"

"Or I can call him and—"

"No, he'll phone here. He wouldn't want to be bothered at roll call and he'll be leaving the station right after. Anyway, Joyce, I've got something important for you to do. An outside errand that'll take you almost all afternoon. That is, if you don't mind doing it."

"Of course not. What is it?"

"It's in connection with the job I just saw a man about. We get it if I can find a close enough match to a certain kind of paper. But I'll have to show him a sample tomorrow morning to get his approval on it, so we won't have time to get samples by mail. Wait, I'll show you the paper."

He went back to the stock room and returned with a piece of light green calendared paper which he handed Joyce.

"That's the stuff," he said. "You see, a couple of years ago I printed him a catalog on that kind of paper. Now he wants a supplement, and wants the paper to match—as near as possible—in weight, shape, texture, surface, all down the line. But the mill that made that stuff's gone out of business.

"So I want you to take that sample around to as many paper companies here as you can cover this afternoon. Show it to them and get a sample from each of them of the closest match to it they can make. Understand?"

"Of course, Mr. Conn. And you want prices?"

"Right. Thirty-five reams of seventeen-by-twenty-two. Get the quotations on that quantity. And that's, for a shop like this, a sizable enough order to make it worth while shopping for price. So even if by any chance you run into an exact match on the paper on your first or second try, keep on going the rounds and you might find it again at a better price.

"Take your notebook and a pencil. Fresh page so you can tear it out and take it with you. Ready? Here are the companies I want you to try."

He gave her a dozen of them, four in downtown Los Angeles, the rest scattered.

"You may not be able to cover *all* of those, but get as many as you can. And keep track of your bus fare. Get the downtown ones first—they're the best bets anyway. Oh, and telephone in some time between three and four and let me know how you're doing."

"All right. Shall I go downtown right from lunch?"

He looked up at the clock. "Why don't you leave now? If you're not hungry yet you can take the bus downtown first and eat after you get there. Got enough money for all the bus fares and everything?"

"I think so."

"If you only think so, take ten out of the cashbox. Don't bother leaving a slip for it; we'll straighten it out tomorrow. Now scoot. Sooner you start the more of them you can cover."

Three minutes later he breathed a sigh of relief when the bell of the door tinkled. Moved over and pretended to be working at the counter, from where he could watch the bus stop and see her standing there. Sighed again with even deeper relief when, a few minutes later, he saw her step onto the bus for downtown.

Quickly he wrote a sign "Back in an hour," stuck it on the inside of the glass of the front door, then locked the door from the inside, went out the back way and to his car.

Right now would be the best time to make the trip to the storage company to get the things he'd need from there. Simplest thing would be to say he'd changed his mind about going away, get both suitcases back intact. Then tomorrow morning after the money from the bank box had been added, after the suitcases contained everything that could connect him with *any* crime, leave them, with the same story, at a different storage company.

And be safe, completely safe. Until then having the suitcases in his car would be only a slight extra risk. Joyce was the real danger, Joyce and her eagerness to tell her story to the police.

He drove as fast as he could drive safely and without risk of being picked up for speeding. Lincoln Boulevard, as usual, was being torn up and he swore at a detour that made him lose minutes.

Thank God he *hadn't* remailed the storage slip to himself after he'd found the bank closed.

He made it back by one-thirty. Opened up the shop, leaving the suitcases locked in the trunk compartment of the car. Then, on second thought, brought them in and put them in the storage closet. If Charlie dropped in he just might remember that he'd once wanted to look through the car that had so recently been Atkins'. He'd rather not have Charlie see the suitcases, even though he could have a simple story ready to cover why they were there. Later, Charlie would remember them, and it would be one more thing.

It was going to be a tough afternoon, he knew, looking around him and wondering what job to tackle first. He'd have to do Joyce's work as well as his own. And tomorrow, too, damn it, and for as many days as it would take him to find a new girl to take Joyce's place. Joyce was a good worker, too; he'd have lots of grief before he'd find another one as efficient. Why had she had to know Atkins and make a date with him?

The phone call from her came at a quarter to four. She'd made the four downtown stops and three others. She was on her way to the eighth place, in Culver City.

"Are you near it now, Joyce?"

"Just got off the bus. Two blocks to walk, but I realized it'd be after four if I waited until after I'd been there."

"Okay, Joyce, you go to that one more place and then knock it off. If you go home from there you'll get home about the same time you usually do, or a little sooner. Any luck?"

"All of them have had something *fairly* close and I've got

two samples that are so much like it that you can hardly tell the difference. Do you want the prices?"

"No, you can tell me tomorrow morning when you give me the samples. Just make that one more place you're through for the day. I'll see you at nine in the—Oh, say, Barrett was here and left a message for you."

"Yes, Mr. Conn?"

"He won't be able to see you this evening as he planned. But he'll put you on the top of his order of business for tomorrow. He asked what time you went to lunch and when I told him he said if it was all right by you he'd like to be in then and take you out to lunch so you'll have plenty of time to talk."

"Gee, that's swell."

"Yeah, you'll have a free meal out of it too. And one more thing. He told me to ask you if you've talked to anybody else—anybody besides me—about Claude Atkins and your date with him."

"Why no, I haven't, Mr. Conn. I was so busy over the week end, moving and everything, I didn't see any of my friends. And besides, it wasn't until late yesterday evening that I read the paper and—"

"That's fine, Joyce. He said to tell you not to talk to anybody else before you talk to him. I haven't got the faintest idea why and I didn't bother to ask him, but he must have some reason. Anyway, I'm passing the message on. So long; see you tomorrow morning."

"Good-by, Mr. Conn. I won't talk to anybody about it."

It had been a bright idea, he thought as he put down the receiver, to tell Joyce that. He felt fairly sure from Joyce's story as she told it to him this morning that she hadn't talked to anybody about it yet; she'd been alone in her room and it had been late evening, too late, she'd said, for her to go to the police that night, and before then there'd been nothing much to talk about.

But this evening she'd be free and might look up a friend or friends. It wouldn't matter if she told them she'd had a date with a man who had been murdered (the police would find out about that anyway) but telling that much might lead to the whole story, or enough of it to mean trouble.

At five he closed the shop and went to eat. Hungry,

because he'd had only a sandwich for lunch and had eaten it early.

Started home after a fair dinner at the Broken Drum (Can't Be Beat) on Wilshire near Lincoln.

Realized there was no reason for him to go home and that he shouldn't. Work at the shop was almost hopelessly behind already and with Joyce gone things would get worse before they could get better. And the shop counted plenty now, because, with the additional complication of having to kill Joyce, it would be a long, long time before it would be safe for him to resume the Plan, even to the extent of realizing on some of the bills he'd already made.

No reason why he shouldn't go back to the shop and work late, as long as he could work without tiring himself out too much. Until midnight or longer, if he could. As well do that as kill time at home, waiting.

Back at the shop he pulled down the blinds, as he always did when working after hours when the shop wasn't supposed to be open, and made sure both doors were locked before he went to Joyce's desk for the checkbook. Might as well get that over with now, eliminating the stub of the check she'd written for Atkins. He hadn't wanted to do that during the afternoon, while Charlie might have dropped in, but it was safe now. Even if someone did come the locked doors would give him time to get the book out of sight.

Luck was with him, he knew when he saw that the last check Joyce had written, the one for Atkins, had been the first check in a fresh filler. He wouldn't have to extricate the stub and get a blank stub-with-check in its place. He took the whole filler out and put a fresh one in its place. Carried over the total, in his own handwriting, not trying to imitate Joyce's since each of them wrote checks.

He took the filler with the Atkins stub back to the storage closet and put it in one of the suitcases.

As simple as that. No check, no stub. By tomorrow, no Joyce to tell about it. No possible evidence against him anywhere but in two suitcases safe in storage.

Let them try to prove anything on him, anything at all.

He went back to the Linotype to turn on the heat under the melting pot and saw that he'd forgotten to turn it off when he'd left. Good thing he'd come back, although it wouldn't have mattered except to run up his bill for electricity a few dollars.

But every few dollars was going to count now for a while.

He sighed and put copy on the clip board. Fingers to the keyboard.

42×81 in. Rayon Marquisette CURTAIN PANELS . . . Ivory only . . . trim up those windows now with this Chaney special value . . . hurry . . . EACH

His name was Death, and he waited for Darius Conn.

Alone in a dark room he sat on the edge of a bed. Beside him ready to his right hand a revolver, ready to his left a flashlight.

Before him, ten feet away, the dim gray rectangle of a window, invitingly wide open to a fire escape. Invitation to Darius Conn.

If there was a sound at the door he could easily change his plan but he hoped and thought it was the fire escape that Conn would use. The girl had said, early this evening, that she'd told Conn about it.

Come on, damn you, he thought. Come on, come on. It's after two. What are you waiting for?

The faint scrape. The faint silhouette against the gray rectangle. The waiting pause, the listening. The stoop, and the step inside. Wait for two or three more steps, let him get close enough, then—

The flashlight speared the dark and caught Darius Conn, caught him in mid-step, changed whatever expression had been on his face to sudden shock, pulled a gasp out of him. A ridiculous Conn, who had attempted to disguise himself. Yes, as he'd guessed from the descriptions, elevator shoes, padded shoulders, something to distend his mouth and make the lower part of his face wider, probably wax inside his mouth. Sloppy, amateur stuff.

"Hi, Darry," he said quietly. In his ordinary tone of voice so Conn would know it.

"Charlie!" Hardly more than a whisper, but Conn looked deflated after it, deflated as though it had let the air out of him, all of the air.

"There's a gun on you," Barrett said. "Don't try for yours

if you've got one. Have you got one, Darry?"

"Yes. In my pocket. All right, you've got me, Charlie."

"You son of a bitch," Barrett said.

Conn's voice was tired, and he looked tired. "I said you've got me. Why rub it in?"

"You bastard. *Why* do you think I've got you?"

"Does it matter why? I slipped somewhere, I guess."

"Slipped somewhere? Hell, I've been only a jump behind you all along. I knew you killed Atkins and Harper when I talked to you Saturday. I guessed why. I knew you were counterfeiting. I've known it for months. I put the idea in your mind."

He saw, and liked, the look on Conn's face. That distorted face, that hated face.

Conn said, "I don't get— Why didn't you—?"

"Because I've been waiting for this. I've waited a year, Darry. Do you think I wanted you in jail for counterfeiting, where I couldn't get you?"

Still bewilderment. Good. The better when it came.

He said very quietly, "Darry, you thought you got away with murder a year ago. Didn't it ever dawn on you that *one* man knew that the man with Myrtle that night didn't kill her, and that you did?"

It came now, the look on Conn's face that he'd been waiting for. He savored it.

He said, "I could have testified then, Darry, and got you the chamber. I might have lost my job—but probably not even that. But I waited because I wanted—this."

He said, "I'll get away with it, Darry. I split up with Kuzwa, left him to guard the Dugan girl and convinced him I could handle you easier alone. And I can, Darry. Only don't think I'm going to arrest you."

He said, "I loved Myrtle. It wasn't just a toss in the hay. I was trying to get her to leave you and she would have. You murdered her. God damn you, God damn you."

Conn was swaying, looking as though he might fall, might throw up.

He couldn't wait much longer. He said, "You son of a bitch. Here it is."

He pulled the trigger twice.

Used the flash to find the light switch and turned it on.

Walked back to the still thing that had been Darius Conn

and felt for a heartbeat that wasn't there. Wrapped a handkerchief around his hand to take Conn's revolver from Conn's pocket and wrap a dead hand around it.

Walked to the door and opened it to tumult outside. Girls in robes over sleeping garments. Someone dialing at the telephone in the middle of the hallway. They shrank back from him.

He said, "It's all right, girls. Joyce is all right; she wasn't in her room. I was there to trap a prowler; he resisted and I was forced to shoot."

Walked confidently down the hallway toward the phone. "If that's the department you just dialed, let me talk when they answer."

About the Author

Fredric Brown wrote 28 novels, 22 of which were crime novels. His short stories appeared in over a score of magazines, mostly detective and science fiction, and several have been adapted for television shows like "Alfred Hitchcock Presents," "Star Trek," and "The Outer Limits." Fredric Brown died in 1972 and, in an irony common to his generation of writers, has come into much critical acclaim since his death.